How to Fall For a Rockstar

Rockstar

Cash & the Sinners #3
D.E. Haggerty

A Valentine for Valerie
A Love for Lexi
About Face
At Arm's Length
Hands Off
Knee Deep
Molly's Misadventures

Chapter 1

Leia – a single mom who doesn't have time for a bass player who thinks he can tell her how to be a parent no matter how sexy he is

LEIA

I smile as I dump the last box on the porch. It's taken me a month to unpack all of our boxes but it's done. Isla and I finally have our very own home.

It's been more than eleven years since my daughter's birth but I did it. I've fulfilled my dream. I have a job that challenges me and pays the bills. And we have our own adorable little house in the small town of Winter Falls.

I tilt my head back and enjoy the view of the Rocky Mountains in the distance. I inhale and breathe in the crisp, fresh air. Isla and I are going to be very happy living here.

The door flies open behind me. "There you are."

I ruffle Isla's hair. "Was I lost?"

She rolls her eyes. Those blue eyes are the exact same shade as mine. Her blonde curly hair is the same as mine as well. She's my mini-me. The only trait she has from her father is her height. She's nearly as tall as me already. Which isn't saying much since I'm barely five feet tall.

"Are you done?" Isla asks.

"Done with what?"

She motions toward the boxes. "Housework."

I snort. I'm a single mom. I'm never done with housework. "Maybe," I hedge.

"Good. Let's play." Subtlety doesn't work on my daughter. It never has.

I still need to break down these boxes and haul them to the recycling center. I also need to finish a load of laundry, do the dishes, and clean the bathroom. And those are just my household chores.

I also have a ton of work from my boss, Brody Bragg. Being the personal assistant of a brilliant game developer with his own company is more than a full-time job. And Brody does not help matters. He assigns me tasks but never provides me with the information I need to complete them.

We've had more than one argument. If my life was a romance novel, he'd be the grumpy boss I fall in love with. But this isn't a romance novel. Plus, Brody's in love with Soleil, the mother of his daughter, Meadow, and he lives with them. Unlike my baby daddy who couldn't escape quick enough once Isla was born.

I shove all thoughts of how demanding my boss can be and how much boring housework I have to do out of my mind. It's a beautiful Saturday afternoon and I'm finally finished unpacking. We should be celebrating.

"What do you want to play?"

Isla beams up at me. "Tag."

I groan. I hate playing tag and she knows it. Whereas my daughter loves to run, I hate it. When your legs are short stumps, running is no fun. As I discovered in high school when I thought joining the cross-country team was a great way to make friends my freshman year. It wasn't.

"This porch is home base," she says. "And you can't stand here and wait for me." She darts off to hide before I have the chance to protest.

I turn around to count to fifty. *One, two, three...*

"You have to count out loud!"

I start again. "One, two, three..."

I hit fifty and whirl around. "Ready or not, here I come!"

I hear a giggle near the side of the house. My daughter loves to play tag but she sucks at hiding. She thinks being a fast runner means she doesn't need to hide well. She isn't wrong.

I pretend to search the area and circle the house in the other direction. As soon as I'm out of her view, I start running as fast as I can which, admittedly, isn't very fast.

I race all the way around the house until I'm directly behind Isla. I slow and tiptoe toward her. I've nearly reached her when she glances behind and sees me.

"Gotcha!"

She squeals and dashes away. She doesn't aim for home base, though. Not my daughter. She wants me to chase her around the yard. Since I can never say no to my girl, I do.

"I'm going to get you!"

She throws her hands in the air and giggles. "You can't catch me!"

Probably not, but I don't give up. She nears the street and I accelerate until I'm sprinting as fast as I can.

"Don't go in the street!"

A man rushes out of the house next door and runs to Isla. She screeches to a halt in front of him. I slow down but I can't stop. My legs are not under my control. I slam into the man and we topple to the ground.

"I'm sorry." I scramble to get off of him.

"Oof! Careful where you put your knee."

I look down and realize my knee is in his crotch. My face heats and I quickly put all my weight on my other knee causing me to tilt over and fall on the grass.

"Mom!" Isla kneels next to me. "Are you okay?"

"I'm fine." Embarrassed but fine.

The man scowls at me. "This is your daughter?"

Here we go again. I got pregnant with Isla when I was seventeen. Some people can be unbelievably judgmental about teenage moms.

I get to my feet and wipe the grass off my jeans and shirt.

"You should be more careful," the man growls.

I fist my hands on my hips and face off with him. I open my mouth to give him a piece of my mind but stop when I catch my first sight of him.

Holy cows have come home and it's time to do some milking! Someone is the definition of sexy. He's tall with broad shoulders, a thick beard, defined cheekbones, and green eyes I want to drown in.

My gaze travels down his body and I can't help but notice how powerfully built he is. Those arms appear strong enough to lift me up and push me against the nearest flat surface. My body warms as I imagine how it would feel to have his hard body pressed against mine.

"Are you listening to me?" he grumbles.

His deep, gruff voice almost has me shivering. I imagine him ordering me around in the bedroom with his gruff voice and my breath stutters in my chest. I want that. I want it bad.

He snaps his fingers in my face. "I'm talking to you."

I clear my throat and force my thoughts away from sexy times with the stranger.

"What did you say?"

"I said," he growls. "You need to watch your daughter better. She could have ended up in the road and gotten hit by a car."

His comment causes my daydream of us sweaty and naked together to vanish. What a jerk! I fist my hands on my hips.

"I know how to care for my daughter."

"Could have fooled me."

"I'm her mom." I slap my chest. "And look around." I wave toward the street. "There are no cars here."

He nods to the house next door where there's a truck parked.

I frown. This is Winter Falls. Trucks and cars are pretty much banned here since the town's claim to fame is being the first carbon neutral town in the world. They are very serious about the environment here.

"You can't own a truck."

"We borrowed it since we're moving in."

"Moving in?"

I knew the house next door was available to rent but I figured it would be a while before anyone rented it. The place has five bedrooms and the rent is five times what I'm paying. Who can afford it?

He crosses his arms over his chest and grunts.

I ignore those muscular arms and concentrate on the problem here. He's going to be living next door. The man who thinks he can tell me how to raise my child. Hold on. Maybe there's a silver lining here. Maybe he has children who are Isla's age.

"Do you have children?"

He grunts again.

"Grunting is not a proper answer."

"No children." He motions to the four men standing on the porch watching our encounter.

He's living with four men? Are they roommates? Are they going to be loud and disrupt Isla's sleep? I didn't move to this small town to have a bunch of frat boys living next to me.

One of the men waves and I realize I recognize him. He's Cash from the rock band *Cash & the Sinners*. I narrow my eyes and study the rest of the men. Holy smoke! It's the entire band.

The man standing in front of me isn't just some grumpy neighbor who thinks he can tell me how to parent my child. My mouth starts to drop open but I snap it shut. I am not fangirling over the grump.

Chapter 2

Fender – a bass player who doesn't know what to do about a woman who doesn't care he's a rockstar

FENDER

> *I'll treasure and protect,*
> *With you, I'll resurrect.*

Cash smiles as he finishes singing the lyrics to our new song *Resurrect.* Cash is the singer and songwriter for the band *Cash & the Sinners. Resurrect* is his favorite number. Not surprising since the song is all about him convincing his high school sweetheart to give him another chance.

Dylan slaps him on the back. He plays lead guitar for the band. He's also sporting a big smile. Probably because he's in love with Virginia, a girl he went to high school with but had forgotten all about. Somehow he managed to convince her to give him a chance.

I frown. Love is fine for the two of them, but I want no part of it. I learned my lesson. Love isn't for me.

A picture of my neighbor, Leia, pops into my mind. The woman is a firecracker wrapped up in a tiny package. She can't be much taller than five feet. She doesn't weigh much either.

Although, I did enjoy the feel of her slight weight on top of me. Until she kneed me in the balls.

Her daughter, Isla, is a copycat of her mom. Blonde curly hair, blue eyes, and a mischievous smile.

Gibson snaps his fingers in front of me. "Earth to Fender. Earth to Fender."

"Ah, leave the poor man alone," Jett says. "He's probably daydreaming about Leia."

"She is one hot mamma." I narrow my eyes at Gibson and he holds up his hands. "Don't worry. I won't steal your woman away."

"Not my woman," I grumble.

Jett and Gibson cackle in response. Why I agreed to live with these two yahoos is beyond me. Gibson is the rhythm guitarist for the band. He's also a charmer who thinks getting a woman to drop her panties in two seconds is his greatest achievement.

Jett isn't much better. He's the drummer and a daredevil who doesn't think twice about racing around a track in a motorbike at 200 miles per hour when he's supposed to be doing a soundcheck.

"She's pretty," Cash chimes in because no one can keep their nose out of my business.

"Fender probably weighs twice what she does. Do you think he'd crush her when they're banging?" Jett asks.

Gibson rolls his eyes. "How long has it been since you got laid? There are a multitude of ways to bang without crushing the woman. Reverse cowgirl is one of my favorites."

If I had Leia in my bed, there's no way we'd be in the reverse cowgirl position. I'd rather gaze into her cheeky blue eyes or watch her tits bounce up and down. Although, I bet staring at her ass as I thrust into her wouldn't be a bad view either.

My pants tighten. I inhale a deep breath and tell my cock to calm down. He won't be inside Leia anytime soon. Or ever.

I'm done with relationships and Leia isn't a one-night stand type of woman. She's the woman you introduce to your family. Too bad for her I have no family worth introducing a woman to.

Jett throws his sticks down and prowls toward Gibson. "I've been laid plenty. I'm probably winning."

I scowl. Jett and Gibson need to stop their stupid competition about who can sleep with the most women. I may not want a relationship but I know better than to use women as pawns in a game. This competition is going to bite them both in the ass.

Dylan steps in between them. "No fighting in the recording studio."

Jett smirks. "But we can fight somewhere else?"

"Come on." Gibson motions to the door. "Let's have a brawl in the middle of Main Street."

"We'll liven things up."

Winter Falls doesn't need livening up. It may be a small town of barely over one-thousand inhabitants but the place is anything but dull. There are pagan festivals at least once a month and visitors from throughout the state of Colorado pack the town during them.

If the festivals didn't already liven the town up, the residents would. To say they're kooky is a major understatement. There's literally a man who walks his squirrels without pants on. Yes, squirrels.

I thought this place was going to be dull when we arrived to record our latest album here. Cash convinced us other bands had recorded at *Bertie's Recording Studio* and we went along with him. Mostly because we all needed a break and a small town seemed a good place for one.

Little did we know he had found out the brothers he never knew about while growing up live here. He's now part of a big family and is settled down in Winter Falls with the love of his life.

"We're not done yet," Stan, our producer, announces over the speaker.

Gibson bounces on his toes and begins shadow boxing. "But we're having a rumble on Main Street."

"Another night in jail won't kill me," Jett declares.

Dylan growls at the reminder of the first night Jett spent in jail here. It was because he scared Dylan's woman, Virginia, to death when he broke into the library where she works.

"Guys," Rob, the studio engineer, calls. "Can we try the song in a different key?"

"Why? It was perfect," Gibson says.

"Mr. Humble has arrived at the party," Jett mumbles but he sits back down behind his drumkit.

We play the song again. For as much bitching as Gibson and Jett do, they are professional when it comes to the music. If they weren't, I'd probably have pushed them off a building by now.

"Whoo-hoo!" Jett twirls his sticks in the air. "We're finally done with this album."

"Not quite," Dylan says.

"Close enough. I can't wait for some time off."

"Are you heading off somewhere?" Cash asks the question I'm thinking.

"There's a surfing competition I want to enter."

Gibson's nose wrinkles. "I thought you quit surfing after the shark bite."

Jett rolls his eyes. "I wasn't the one who got bit by the shark."

Gibson snorts. "Which was a surprise considering how much you screamed like a little girl."

"I did not scream like a little girl."

Their bickering could go on forever. I stand and put my bass away.

"Hungry," I say and aim for the exit.

"Are we doing the brewery or the diner?" Dylan asks as he follows me.

"I vote the brewery. They have the best burgers," Gibson says.

"You just want a beer," Jett says.

I frown. Gibson has been drinking an awful lot lately. Being in a rock band doesn't mean he needs to drink a six-pack every night.

"Let's hit the diner." Cash rubs his stomach. "I'm in the mood for meatloaf and potatoes."

"I'm in." Dylan agrees.

Cash and Dylan always agree. The two were best friends in high school and remain as close as ever. And now the women they're dating are best friends.

I often disagree with them because I can and it irritates them. But in this case, I agree. The diner doesn't have a liquor license.

"The diner it is," I say as I exit the studio and turn toward *Moon's Diner*.

"Race you there," Jett says and sprints away. Gibson is hot on his heels.

"So, Leia," Cash says and I notice he's on one side of me while Dylan's on the other.

I growl. I expect this shit from Tweedle Dum and Tweedle Dee. Not from them.

"She's pretty," Dylan adds.

"Single mom."

I don't need to say more. They know about my feelings for single moms. They know the entire story. They witnessed the fiasco while it played out.

"Not all single moms are the same as—"

My growl cuts him off. I'm not talking about *her*. I'm never talking about *her*.

"You're going to have to get over her at some point."

I glare at Dylan. He holds up his hands.

"Fine. Hold onto a grudge about a woman for the rest of your life. You'll die old and miserable all by yourself."

Good. Alone is how I want to be.

"Leia didn't seem impressed with your rockstar status," Cash says.

I should have known they wouldn't let it go. I increase my pace. Cash and Dylan are tall but they've got nothing on my height of six-foot-six. They have to jog to keep up with me.

"You can't get rid of us," Dylan says.

Cash points to my growling stomach. "You need to eat and you haven't had time to stock your house yet."

My mistake. I'll make certain the house is never devoid of food again. As soon as I figure out a way to stop Gibson and Jett from eating all my food.

"Good afternoon," Petal, an elderly woman who lives in town, greets us as we come upon her.

I don't bother to greet her back. I usually try to be polite to the women in this town but the candle store owner is on a mission where I'm concerned.

"Have you thought about my suggestion?" she asks.

"No."

She pats my arm. The patting quickly becomes petting. I step away from her and she sighs.

"You have time. Sexy book club isn't for a few weeks." She winks at me. "You'd make a great model." She waves as she walks away.

"Model?" Dylan asks.

"According to Indy, they want a man to strip for them at book club." Cash's grin is downright evil. "Fender must be the chosen one."

"Not stripping," I say and continue toward the diner.

"I bet you'd strip for Leia," Cash hollers after me and I give him the finger.

I'm not stripping for Leia. No matter how sexy the little firecracker is. She's off limits to a man like me.

Chapter 3

Pagan festival – an excuse for the town of Winter Falls to throw a party

LEIA

"What's Litha?" Isla asks as we walk toward the town center for the festival. Or, rather, I walk. Isla is skip-running. I keep a death grip on her hand before she gets ahead of me and ends up lost in the crowd.

"It's the summer solstice." I think. I didn't exactly read up on pagan festivals before I came to Winter Falls. I didn't realize I needed to.

"I know what it is!" Indigo says as she jogs across the street toward us with Virginia.

Indigo and Virginia are recent arrivals in Winter Falls as well. Indigo decided her and Virginia are my new best friends. Since I don't exactly have time to make new friends, I didn't complain about her declaration.

"Is this Isla?" Virginia asks.

"Isla, meet my friend Virginia."

Isla waves to her while Virginia bounces on her toes.

"She's adorable! She's your mini-me."

No matter how many times someone says Isla is my carbon copy, I'll never get tired of hearing it. Of hearing how my daughter doesn't resemble *him.*

"Do you know what Litha is?" Isla asks Indigo since she doesn't enjoy being reminded of how much she resembles her mom.

"It marks an important transitional moment in the Earth's seasonal cycle. Fertile energy is at its peak and new life is rapidly growing," Indigo says. I assume she knows since she's a fourth-grade teacher at the local school.

"How do you celebrate Litha?" I ask.

Indigo shrugs and Virginia raises her hands. "Don't ask me. My boss, Gratitude, pretty much refuses to explain any local traditions to me. I'm apparently just supposed to know them."

Virginia is the local librarian. She's taking over from Gratitude assuming the elderly lady ever agrees to retire. Thus far, she's refusing to so much as slow down.

"I guess we'll see," Indigo sings. She grabs Isla's hand, and they skip ahead of us toward Main Street.

"How are …" My question trails off when we reach the town square.

Two poles are set up in the middle of the square with a pile of hay in between them. There's a long line of people standing on one side of the square. What's going on here?

"What are they waiting for?" Virginia asks.

"Let's go find out."

"Um…" She glances around the square and the crowd of people.

I grasp her hand and drag her along. "There's no reason to be scared."

She scowls at me. "Being shy doesn't mean I'm scared."

"Good because I think this is a competition of some sort."

I spot Indigo and Isla and head toward them.

"It's a contest." Indigo indicates the poles. "Whoever jumps the highest wins."

"I'm going to win," Isla declares.

Pride fills me. My girl has no fear.

"Where do we sign up?" I scan the area and notice a woman with a clipboard standing at the front of the line of people. I take Isla's hand and march there while Virginia and Indigo stay at the back of the line.

"Is this where we sign up for the hay jumping contest?"

The woman's lips purse. "It's not a hay jumping contest. It's a bonfire jumping contest."

Crap. I'm all about being the mom who allows her daughter to explore her boundaries but there's no way I'm allowing her to jump over fire. Temper tantrum here we come.

"There's no fire," Isla points out.

"Correct. Bonfires are banned in Winter Falls as they're bad for the environment." Before I can ask how a bonfire is bad for the environment, she continues, "The hay simulates fire."

Phew. "Can I sign my daughter up here?"

"You can, but you're not going to win," a woman behind us says.

My brow wrinkles. "Do I know you?"

She sticks out her hand. "I'm Ashlyn. I own *Bertie's Recording Studio.*" I shake her hand but I must appear confused – probably because I am – because she continues, "Where *Cash & the Sinners* are recording their latest album."

A vision of Fender pops into my mind. Too bad the bass player is a grumpy asshole who thinks he can tell me how to raise my child. If he weren't, I'd want to explore every inch of those strong muscles of his.

You do want to explore every inch of him.

I ignore my inner voice. She enjoys getting me in trouble. Pregnant at seventeen, remember?

Which is why you googled the band after meeting Fender.

My inner voice isn't merely a troublemaker. She's also a shit stirrer. It's best I ignore her.

"I'm Leia," I finally manage to tell Ashlyn.

"I know. You're Brody's new personal assistant." She gestures toward the woman with the clipboard. "This is my sister, Lilac. She resembles a robot but she's actually made of flesh and blood. I checked."

Lilac rolls her eyes at her sister and Isla giggles. Ashlyn winks at her. "And you must be Isla."

"I'm going to win the contest."

Ashlyn narrows her eyes at my daughter. "I'm the reigning champion. Think you can beat me?"

Isla studies Ashlyn. Unlike me, Ashlyn's tall. My daughter isn't intimidated, though. She merely straightens her back and tilts her chin up.

"Sign me up, too," Indigo says as she joins us.

I glance her way and notice she's not alone. In addition to Virginia, the entire band is with her – including the king of grumps. I don't pay any attention to him, though. Nope. I have no interest in him whatsoever.

My phone vibrates in my pocket. I dig it out and scowl. *Brody calling.*

"I need to answer this. Can you keep an eye on Isla?" I ask Indigo.

Indigo salutes. "Aye, aye, Captain."

I shake my head at her antics as I walk away to find a quiet place to answer my phone. I end up in an alley between the library and *Eden's Garden,* the local flower shop.

"Make it quick," I order as I answer the phone.

I probably shouldn't give my boss orders but Brody drives me bonkers. How he ever managed to capture Soleil's heart is beyond me.

Brody rattles off a bunch of stuff he needs me to do this very minute. I roll my eyes. He's crazy if he thinks I'm working on a Saturday afternoon when there's a town festival. I don't kowtow to any man.

"Yeah, yeah," I murmur. "Send me an email with a list and I'll work on it."

Notice how I didn't promise to finish anything today. I wasn't born yesterday.

I hang up the phone and make my way to the end of the alley. When I reach it, Fender steps out of the shadows to block me.

"Excuse me." I try to scoot around him but he crosses his arms over his chest and refuses to budge. "What's your problem?"

"It's a holiday."

I'm fairly certain Litha isn't an actual holiday but whatever.

"You shouldn't be working."

"I'm not, grumpapottamus."

"Grumpapottamus?" a man asks from behind him. "Love it. I hereby christen Fender Grumpapottamus."

Another man shoves Fender out of the way. "I'm Jett." He waggles his eyebrows. "I'm the best band member."

I cock an eyebrow. "Band member?"

I know exactly who he is. He's the drummer for *Cash & the Sinners*. And the other man is Gibson, the rhythm guitarist for the band. But I'm not giving them the satisfaction of going all crazed fan on them. Their egos are probably bigger than the state of Colorado as it is.

Gibson chuckles. "She's perfect."

Fender growls at him.

"What's wrong, grumpapottamus?" Jett teases.

I giggle. I think I might like Jett.

"Don't you have a drum circle dance to get to?" Fender asks.

Jett's eyes pop open. "Shit. I'm late." He runs away but doesn't get far before whipping around and coming back. "Nice to meet you, Leia, mother of Isla." He bows before rushing away again.

"By the way, I'm Gibson." Gibson holds out his hand but instead of shaking mine, he kisses my fingers. Fender growls and Gibson winks at me before following Jett.

"This was fun but I need to get back to the jumping competition." I don't wait for a response from Fender before marching away. Unfortunately, he doesn't get the hint and follows me. I ignore him.

I also force myself to ignore the heat coming off his body reaching out to me and the scent of his musky cologne tickling my nose. I refuse to swoon over some grumpy jerk who thinks he can tell me what to do. I'll work whenever I want to, thank you very much.

"Mom!" Isla waves me over.

I dismiss Fender as we get closer to my daughter. "You may leave now."

He grunts.

"I don't speak grunt, grumpy dude."

"You shouldn't abandon your daughter with strangers."

Abandon? What does he know about abandoning someone? I have had it with this guy. What is his problem? He needs to mind his own business.

"I did not abandon my child. I would never abandon her. I left her with Indigo who is my friend. She's not a stranger. Guess what else it is?" I pause but he doesn't fill in the blanks. "It's none of your business." I make a shooing motion. "Now go away and join your friends or, I don't know, jump off the cliffs at Winter Falls. I don't care as long as you leave."

His nostrils flare and his mouth opens. I wait for whatever garbage he's going to spew next. But he doesn't speak. He huffs before turning on his heel and stomping away. Good. Let him go have his man temper tantrum elsewhere. I'm busy here.

Isla yanks on my hand. "Mom. I'm next. Watch me."

"You got this, baby girl."

She sprints toward the hay and I clap to encourage her. What I don't do is scan the area for Fender. Nope. I'm pushing the man and his obnoxiously strong body out of my mind.

I don't need a man. I don't want a man. I am not risking history repeating itself.

Chapter 4

Play – something children do but it's even better when you're an adult

FENDER

"Why don't you go over there already?"

At Gibson's question, I drag my gaze away from Leia's house. I could lie to myself and say I didn't realize I was staring at her house but I prefer not to lie.

The little firecracker fascinates me. I wonder if her blonde hair would feel like silk in my hands. Is her skin soft to the touch? Do those mischievous blue eyes sparkle when she's turned on?

Too bad she has relationship written all over her. And there's also the small matter of the two of us fighting whenever we're in the same room.

"Or are you chicken?" Jett asks before he begins bwaking. "Bwak. Bwak."

"Maybe he just needs some tips on how to seduce a lady." Gibson rubs his hands together. "I am happy to assist you with this endeavor."

I glare at him.

"Glare at me all you want, grumpapottamus. I know you're a big softie inside."

I give him the finger.

"If you don't want Gibson's help, I'm available. My schedule's wide open."

I frown. Jett and boredom is not a good combination. The adrenaline junkie will need another hit soon and I'm afraid of what the people of Winter Falls will do when he marches down Main Street in his birthday suit while playing *Smells Like Teen Spirit* on his marching snare drum.

"I don't need any help." I head toward the stairs but a knock on the back door has me veering in the opposite direction.

"Hi!" Isla greets when I open the door. "Do you want to come outside and play with me?"

I frown. "Does your mom know where you are?"

She huffs. "I'm eleven and a half."

"You didn't answer my question, kid."

She scrunches up her eyes and scowls at me. It's freaking adorable.

"I'm not a kid." She stomps her foot.

"I can't play with you if you don't have permission from your mom."

"I'll be back." She hurries away. I contemplate shutting the door but I want to be certain she asks Leia for permission instead of pretending.

She dashes into her house but less than a minute later she's back outside. Leia follows her. She glances across our yards and waves to me before turning and hurrying back inside.

I frown. Does Isla want to play with me because her mom doesn't have time for her?

"I have permission!" Isla screams from across her backyard to me.

"What do you want to play?" I ask when she reaches me.

"Yeah," Gibson chimes in. "What do you want to play?"

"Don't forget me." Jett pushes me out of the way to stand on the back porch.

Isla inches closer to me before asking, "Who are they?"

"I'm Gibson."

"And I'm Jett."

"We're friends of Fender."

Isla glances up at me for confirmation. "They're my roommates."

"Are they in the band with you?" I nod. "Are they rockstars, too?"

I nod.

"Okay." She shrugs as if meeting rockstars is not a big deal.

"Let's play Simon says. I'm Simon," she says before she starts bossing everyone around. "Fender, you here. Gibson, you there. Jett, over there."

Once we're in the positions she wants us in, she stands in front of us and places her hands on her hips. She's adorable. The perfect daughter.

A pain knifes through my stomach but I ignore it. Children are not for me. I've learned my lesson. I force thoughts of *her* and the past out of my mind. I prefer not to give any headspace to *her*.

"Simon says touch your left ear."

We touch our left ears.

"Simon says touch your right ear."

We touch our right ears.

Leia points to Gibson. "Simon didn't say to stop touching your left ear. You're out."

"No fair," he pouts.

"Simon says release your ears."

Jett and I drop our hands.

"Simon says touch your toes."

Jett groans. "What if we can't touch our toes?"

Isla cackles. "Simon didn't say you can talk. You're out!"

"This game is harder than I remember." He falls to the ground in a heap. "I'll win the next one."

Isla smiles at me. "You win!"

"The first time the big guy's won anything in a long time," Gibson grumbles, and I give him the finger from behind my back.

Isla hugs me. "Congrats!"

The knife in my chest returns. All I've ever wanted is children of my own. But it's not to be. I pat Isla on the back before stepping out of her hold. Best not to get too attached to someone else's child. Especially when that someone else pisses me off on a regular basis.

"What game is next?" Jett asks.

"Hide and seek. You're it!" Isla tags me before darting away.

Jett and Gibson rush away as well. I sigh before turning around and beginning to count to fifty.

From the corner of my eye, I notice Isla hide behind the trash can next to the porch. I swallow my laughter and continue to count.

"Fifty! Ready or not. Here I come," I shout.

I scan the yard for any sign of Gibson or Jett, but I don't spot them. Not surprising since Gibson is adept at hiding. He's had lots of practice hiding from pissed off fans.

My personal favorite was when he tried hiding in the catering cart but fell out as they were wheeling it toward our suite. Probably because he drank several of the mini bottles of whiskey while he was in there.

"Isla, time for dinner!" Leia hollers from across the yards.

"But we're playing hide and seek," Isla calls from her hiding spot.

I wait for Leia to get angry with Isla for disobeying her. For her to start shouting nasty words at her daughter. My hands fist and my chest heaves. I can't hit a woman but I will ensure Isla is safe.

Leia marches over to our yard. "Here are your choices, daughter of mine." Her gaze travels around the yard as if we don't all know Isla is 'hiding' behind the trash can.

"You can finish your game of hide and seek."

"Yes!" Isla shouts.

"And eat your spaghetti cold when you're finished. Or, you can come out and eat your dinner while it's warm."

"Cold spaghetti is gross," Isla grumbles.

"I give up!" Jett cries as he climbs down the tree.

"I'm hungry," Gibson says as he crawls out from underneath the back porch.

My stomach rumbles in agreement. I check the time and realize it's after six.

Leia bites her lip. "Do you want to come over for dinner?"

Isla abandons her 'hiding spot' to tug on my hand. "Yeah, Fender. Come to dinner."

"Go ahead, Fender. We've got plans," Gibson says.

"What pla—" Gibson elbows Jett before he can finish his question. "Yes, of course. We have other plans. You go along, Fender. Enjoy your spaghetti." He waggles his eyebrows.

"Sorry, squirt." I tweak her nose. "I'm busy."

Leia lets out a visible sigh of relief. She doesn't want to be around me? Same, firecracker, same.

"Come on, Isla." Leia grasps her daughter's hand. "Thank the guys for playing with you this afternoon."

"Thanks for playing with me."

Jett winks. "Anytime, doll face. Anytime."

"Knock on our door whenever you want," Gibson adds.

Leia groans. "You're going to regret those words."

I scowl. "Why? You don't enjoy playing with your own kid?"

She rears back. "What's with the accusation? I meant my Isla has the energy of ten chihuahua puppies who were given espresso for breakfast."

Isla giggles. "Mom's silly. Everyone knows puppies can't have coffee."

Leia wraps her arm around her daughter. "Come on, daughter of mine who knows entirely too much about a puppy she'll never have. Let's go eat."

"Bye!" Isla waves as they walk across the yard.

"You've got your work cut out with her." Jett slaps me on the shoulder.

"Don't worry. We've got your back." Gibson slaps my ass on his way inside the house.

"I don't need your help."

Jett chuckles. "Um, yeah, you do."

"No," I snarl.

Gibson shakes his finger at me. "Don't you worry, grumpa-pottamus. Jett and Gibson are on the job."

"I'm an excellent wingman," Jett proclaims.

"He is," Gibson agrees. "He's been my wingman for years."

Jett shoves him. "I'm not your wingman. But I'll be Fender's."

The two numbskulls can argue about the traits of a wingman all they want. I don't need a wingman. I don't want a woman.

And I certainly don't want Leia. No matter how much my fingers long to thread through her blonde curly locks of hair whenever she's near. My cock twitches in my pants. He wants in on the action. He'll have to settle for my hand.

Chapter 5

Gossip gals – five elderly women who enjoy confusing the snot out of new residents of Winter Falls

LEIA

I enter *Bake Me Happy* with Isla where she announces to the man behind the counter, "I get a treat because I did good today."

"What did you do?" he asks.

"I helped the little kids learn their ABCs." Isla beams and my stomach warms with pride.

Any guilt about forcing her to attend activities at the community center all day during the summer vacation while I work disappears. She's having fun and learning stuff. She's okay. No. She's more than okay. She's thriving. Moving to Winter Falls was the right decision.

"What do you want for a treat, Isla?" the man asks and I gasp. How does he know her name? We've never been inside this bakery before.

He winks at me. "There is no such thing as privacy in Winter Falls, Leia Wilson, personal assistant to Brody Bragg."

I knew small town living would be different. But this is crazy. Before I have a chance to figure out a response, he speaks again, "And I'm Bryan. This is my place."

A man nearly as big as Fender enters the bakery from the kitchen. "No, it isn't."

Bryan rolls his eyes. "I allow him to think he's the boss of me."

"Because I am the boss of you."

Bryan leans over the counter to whisper to me. "He thinks he's the boss of me because he signs my paychecks."

I giggle. "I think signing your paycheck is the definition of boss."

"Who are you?" Isla asks the big guy.

He comes around the counter and kneels in front of her. "I'm Rowan. I have a daughter but she's not as big as you. She's a baby."

"I'm not a baby. I'm eleven and a half."

"And you're here for a treat."

She grins. "Mom said I can have a treat because I was good today."

I place my hand on her shoulder. "She was very good today."

The door opens behind us and someone shouts, "They're in here!"

I glance around but besides Rowan and Bryan, there are no other customers in the bakery other than Isla and myself.

Rowan holds out his hand to Isla. "Do you want a tour of the kitchen where all the baking happens?"

Isla looks up at me with wide eyes. "Can I, Mom? Can I?"

"Trust me, girl," Bryan says before I have a chance to answer. "You want your girl out of firing range."

"Firing range? What's happening?" And do I need to grab my daughter and bolt?

"Everything's fine. Bryan's a bit dramatic," Rowan says before addressing my daughter again. "Come on, Isla. I'm baking some snickerdoodles. How do you feel about cinnamon?"

"Yummy!" she yells before following him to the kitchen.

"Leia Wilson!"

I startle at the sound of my name. Bryan slides a drink across the counter. "Sorry, I don't have any alcohol. A caramel mocha latte will have to do."

Why do I need alcohol? What is happening?

I take a fortifying sip of my drink before slowly facing the woman who called my name. Except it's not one woman. It's five elderly women.

I steel my spine. If I can take my final in business economics smelling of puke after being awake all night with Isla projectile vomiting, I can handle a bunch of old ladies. Side note – I aced that final.

"Hello."

"I'll do the introductions," the woman in the front says. "I'm Sage. I'm the leader."

The woman next to her rolls her eyes. "She always says she's the leader. She's not."

Sage bristles. "I am, too."

"Whatever."

I've never heard a woman old enough to be my grandmother grumble whatever before. I bite my tongue to hide my amusement. No matter how crazy a person is, laughing in their face is wrong.

Sage clears her throat. "Anyway, this is Feather, Petal, Cayenne, and Clove. Together we're the…"

"Gossip gals!" They announce together.

I feel as if I should clap. Should I clap?

"Nice to meet you. I'm—"

"Leia Wilson," Sage cuts me off to answer.

Good thing Bryan prepared me for everyone in town knowing my name. Otherwise, I might have grabbed my daughter and ran for the hills.

"How can I help you?"

Cayenne grins. "It's not what you can do for us, but what we can do for you."

Is she paraphrasing JFK? "I think you have the quote wrong."

Clove frowns at Cayenne. "I thought we agreed not to tell her."

"You're just grumpy because we're at *Bake Me Happy* instead of your café," Sage answers.

"Tell me what?" I ask before the two can begin to argue. Something tells me these women argue with each other a lot. And they enjoy it, too.

Petal sighs. "This is going to be my favorite project."

"They're all your favorite projects!" the other women say in unison.

"Are you a musical group?" I ask because they've responded in perfect unison twice now. It's impressive.

Sage lifts her chin. "I did win the karaoke contest at Saffron's funeral."

I must be having some kind of hallucination due to sleep deprivation. I probably fell asleep on my desk. Any moment now I'm going to wake up with an ink stain on my cheek and post-its stuck to my forehead.

Wake up, Leia. Wake up!

Feather cackles. "She thinks she's sleeping. Or maybe she thinks she's in a coma. Remember the book we read where the heroine was in a coma. She fell in love with a man during a coma dream and when she woke up the man was sitting next to her bed but she didn't know who he was. What was the title of it?"

Sage motions to her. "Feather chooses our books for sexy book club."

"You should join us," Feather says. "We meet once a month."

"Sorry. I don't have time to read. I have a full-time job and I'm a single mom."

"You don't have to read the book," Clove says. "We have nibbles and wine and gossip."

"And soon we'll have a stripper," Cayenne adds. "Assuming Fender agrees."

"Fender is going to strip for you?"

The man may be a grump and a half but I wouldn't mind getting a chance to study those muscles with no clothes covering them. Does he have tattoos? Or is his skin ink free? And how does his skin feel? Would it be soft to the touch? Or hard?

"Yes!" Bryan claps. "I want to come if Fender's stripping." He's not the only one.

"Fender isn't going to strip for the sexy book club!" Rowan hollers from the kitchen.

"Don't crush my dreams," Bryan hollers back. "If I can't have you, I'll settle for Fender."

Rowan is an attractive man but he can't hold a candle to Fender. Rowan's a Hershey's chocolate bar. Fender is a Belgian chocolate bonbon.

"It's sexy *book club*," Feather insists. "It's not stripper night at the bookstore. Anyone who attends book club should read the book."

"In which case, I'll reiterate. I'm a single mom. I don't have time to read."

"Where is Isla anyway?" Clove glances around. "I haven't met her yet."

"None of us have met her," Cayenne adds.

They want to meet my daughter? Meanwhile, I'm worried I'm having some type of fever dream. Can a fever dream cause lasting damage? Do I need an MRI scan?

"I've changed the diapers of almost all the inhabitants of Winter Falls. Your Isla will be no exception," Sage declares.

Diaper changing days are over for my daughter. "Isla's eleven."

"Eleven and a half," my daughter yells from the kitchen. She can hear from a room away when it's to her benefit, but when it's time to pick up her toys? She goes deaf.

"Your next child."

Sage is crazy. Straight up crazy. Do not pass go, proceed directly to the looney bin.

"There will be no next child. I'm one and done." Being done with men automatically means no more babies.

"I bet Fender would make cute babies," Feather declares.

I'm not having a fever dream but they are if they think I'm going to have babies with my grumpaholic neighbor. "Fender?"

Bryan comes to stand next to me. "Let me break this down for you." He motions toward the ladies. "The gossip gals are the town's matchmakers."

"Matchmakers?" Do matchmakers still exist? And why does a town of slightly over 1,000 people need matchmakers?

He bumps my hip. "Yes, matchmakers. And they have de-cided—"

"We don't decide," Cayenne interrupts to say. "Fate does."

Bryan clears his throat. "Fate in the form of the gossip gals has decided you should be paired with Fender."

"Um, no. Mr. Grumpy Pants and I are not now, nor will we ever be a couple."

He sighs. "Resistance is futile."

"Talk to my parents. I will resist no matter how much resistance is deemed futile."

He chuckles. "This is going to be fun."

"There will be no fun because there will be no matchmaking. I have no intention of being matched with any man, let alone grumpapottamus."

Petal grins. "I have some candles to make."

"Candles?" Why is she suddenly mentioning candles? Maybe this is a fever dream after all.

"Petal makes sexy candles," Bryan explains.

Candles can be sexy? "Excuse me?"

"You know massage candles, wax play candles."

No, I don't know. My experience with sex is embarrassingly limited. There isn't much time for fun and games between the sheets when you have a small child to care for who thinks 'stay out' is the name of a game and not an order from her mom.

Sage claps her hands. "I believe we've given Ms. Wilson enough to consider. Gossip gals, move out."

She marches to the door and the rest of the women follow her.

"I don't want to be matched," I holler after her. She flicks her hand before exiting the bakery along with her friends.

"Please tell me I'm sleeping."

Bryan laughs. "You're not sleeping and this is the most fun I've had since Dylan chased Virginia."

I know all about how Dylan humiliated Virginia in high school but forgot about it. When he met her again in Winter Falls, he fell hard for her.

But I'm not interested in a romance story of my own. And, judging by the nasty comments Fender has made about my parenting skills, he doesn't want anything to do with me.

Good. I don't want a man.

Maybe moving to Winter Falls wasn't the right decision after all.

Chapter 6

Babysitter – someone who should watch your child; not tell you how to be a parent

FENDER

I sigh as I set my bass down. I hate to admit it, but it's boring without Tweedle Dee and Tweedle Dum around. Plus, I'm worried about what trouble they're getting into. Those two could find trouble in a convent. In fact, I think they have.

My stomach rumbles and I check my watch. Close enough to dinner time. I guess I'll make some food. The thought of food immediately perks me up.

I'm rummaging through the refrigerator when the doorbell rings. My brow wrinkles. Who the hell is ringing the doorbell? Everyone I know in town would barge in without warning.

I shut the refrigerator and march to the front door.

"I'm really sorry," Leia says the second I open the door.

I cross my arms over my chest and glare at her.

"I need to drive to Denver to pick something up for Brody, but I can't find anyone to watch Isla. The community center is already closed. I can't get ahold of Indigo or Virginia. Even the gossip gals – who promised they'd change my children's diapers – are nowhere to be found."

I scratch my beard in confusion. "Isla doesn't wear diapers."

Her daughter frowns. "I'm not a baby."

I raise an eyebrow at Leia but she shakes her head. "It's a long story."

I wait but I guess she's not telling me her long story.

She clears her throat. "Can you babysit Isla? It's only for a few hours. I should be home by ten at the latest."

I glance down at her daughter who looks up at me with wide eyes. Am I supposed to be able to resist those blue eyes? Can anyone resist them? I certainly can't.

"Please, don't make me beg."

I want to hear Leia begging. Preferably while I'm buried deep inside her and she's on the verge of release. My pants tighten and I grunt.

"Is your grunt a yes? I don't know. I don't speak grunt. Or grump for that matter. I should probably learn. Do they have grump interpretation courses?"

She's rambling and flustered. It's adorable. No, not adorable. She's abandoning her child to a man she barely knows. There's nothing adorable about this woman.

"I'll watch her," I growl.

Her shoulders fall with relief. "Thank you."

She squeezes Isla's shoulder. "Be good for Fender. Listen to what he says. No sassing at him."

Isla grins. "I'm always good."

Leia tweaks her daughter's nose. "No, you're not, but I love you no matter what."

"Love you, Mom."

Leia gives Isla a quick hug before waving and rushing off.

Isla bounces on her toes. "What should we do first? Play tag? Or maybe statues?" She glances behind me. "Where are Gibson and Jett?"

I grunt.

"They're not here? No biggie. You're my favorite."

My heart warms at her words. I'd give the world for a daughter like Isla. But it wasn't meant to be. I scowl at the reminder.

Isla marches into the house and scans the room. "Where are your pictures and extra pillows?"

It is pretty bare in here.

"Rental."

"Oh yeah. Mom said you're leaving as soon as your record is finished."

The record is finished and we haven't left yet. I don't know why Gibson and Jett are still here. As for me? I have nowhere to go. Correction. Nowhere I want to go.

My stomach rumbles to remind me I was in the middle of figuring out dinner when Leia arrived with Isla in tow.

"Dinner."

"You don't talk much," Isla says as she follows me to the kitchen. "I don't mind. I can be quiet too. When I want to. I just don't want to very much."

I chuckle. This kid is a hoot.

"Toasted cheese sandwich?"

"I love toasted cheese sandwiches!" She claps. "I can help. I can butter the bread. Mom doesn't let me use the stove, though."

I place the bread on the kitchen counter along with a knife and the butter.

Isla grabs the knife and begins to butter the bread. "We came to Winter Falls from San Diego. Are you from San Diego, too?" She doesn't wait for an answer before continuing to prattle on. "I didn't like San Diego very much. At least, not after my grandparents died. When they were alive, we lived with them."

In other words, Leia relied on her parents to raise her child.

"But they died when I was little. Before I started school. They were old." She shrugs. "It makes sense I guess since they were Mom's grandparents, my big-grandparents."

"I think you mean great-grandparents."

Her nose wrinkles as she thinks about it. "Yeah. I guess. Great-grandparents. I don't know my grandparents. My mom's parents."

"What about your dad's parents?"

"What about them?"

"They're your grandparents, too."

"I guess."

"Where's your dad?" I ask when she doesn't elaborate and because I'm curious. What happened to the man Leia made this child with? Where is he? Why isn't he here tending to their child while Leia works herself to death?

"I don't know."

Her answer brings up even more questions. But I don't ask any of them. Pumping Isla for information about Leia is wrong. Plus, I don't want information about the firecracker next door.

I grab the bread from Isla. "I think we have enough butter since you used the entire stick."

She giggles. "Did not."

I place two slices of bread in the pan and top them with two slices of cheese each before placing more bread on top.

"Drink?" I ask Isla as I open the refrigerator.

"Water, please. I'm not allowed juice or soda. And milk is gross." She wrinkles up her nose.

I grab a gallon of milk and wave it at her. "Milk it is."

She feigns retching. "Yuck."

"Milk helps you grow."

"Mom already says I grow faster than a beanpole. She blames my dad. I guess he was tall. I don't know. I don't remember him. I saw a picture of him in Mom's yearbook once, but he was sitting down."

"Did your dad go to high school with your mom?" I guess I'm not done asking questions about her dad after all.

"I guess. Mom doesn't talk about him. She gets mad when I ask questions."

She does? Why? I force those thoughts away. I don't want to know.

"Go sit at the table."

Isla doesn't stop chattering away the entire time we eat our dinner. I'm surprised she manages to eat her sandwich.

When we finish, she picks up her plate without me asking and takes it to the sink with her glass.

"What now?"

I shrug. I don't exactly have any children's games in the house.

"We can play cards," she suggests.

"What game?" I ask as I assume she doesn't mean poker. The band plays a ton of poker when we're bored on the road.

"Snap!"

"What's snap?" I ask although I know the game.

"Don't worry." She pats my arm. "It's easy. I'll explain."

I dig around in the kitchen drawers until I find a deck of cards.

"I'm going to win!" Isla squeals. She can win all she wants if her winning makes her this happy. Seeing her happy makes me happy.

"Cheat," I say fifteen minutes later when she has almost the entire deck on her pile.

"Don't be a sore loser. Mom says sore losers don't get dessert. Do you want dessert?"

I grin as I stand. What a little conniver. "I have cookies."

I find the package of chocolate chip cookies and bring them to the living room. Isla grabs the television remote control.

"Mom says too much television rots the brain, but I'm allowed an hour of TV before I go to bed." She widens her eyes at me. "Do you want to watch TV?"

As if I can say no now. I grunt.

"You grunt a lot. It's probably why Mom calls you Mr. Grumpy Pants. I don't think she means your pants are grumpy. I think she means you're a grump."

She switches on the television. "Do you watch this show?"

I don't know what this show is.

"Do you have a television on your touring bus? Or do you read? I can't read while I'm in the car. I get car sick. Mom listens to podcasts. They're boring. I usually fall asleep. How do you sleep in your touring bus?"

She increases the volume on the television. "Commercial's over."

To my surprise, she's actually quiet during the show. I glance over to check on her and realize she's fallen asleep.

There aren't any blankets on the couch, so I grab one off of my bed and cover her with it. When I sit down next to her, she cuddles into my side.

I sigh as I gaze down at her. Cuddling with a daughter of my own is everything I ever wanted but it will never happen. Women always betray you.

Chapter 7

Put your foot in your mouth – When you say things you should know better than to say

LEIA

I fly past a car parked perpendicular to the highway. Crap. Was it a cop car? I glance down at the odometer. I'm going eighty. Fifteen miles over the speed limit.

Brody's fancy car makes it too easy to speed. I barely notice how fast I'm going. Too bad 'I barely noticed how fast I'm going' won't get me out of a speeding ticket.

My hands squeeze the steering wheel. Getting a ticket will slow me down more than driving the speed limit. I force myself to lift my foot from the pedal. Five over the speed limit, I negotiate with myself.

I hate how I had to leave my daughter with Fender. A man who can barely stand the sight of me. He already thinks I'm a bad parent. And now he probably thinks even worse of me.

But what else was I supposed to do? Force Isla to ride in the car with me to Denver and back? She gets car sick. She would have been miserable.

I would have preferred to have any other person in Winter Falls care for my baby girl, but there was no one else. Not one single person answered their phone when I rang them. I'd say it was a conspiracy except I'm certain my life is not important enough to build a whole conspiracy around.

By the time I reach the town limits of Winter Falls, my hands hurt from gripping the steering wheel and my jaw is aching from how clenched it is.

I blow out a breath and slow to the speed limit. Nearly there. A few more minutes and my baby will be in my arms again.

Note to self. If I ever ask someone I barely know to babysit again, get their phone number so I can check in from time to time.

I'm barely stopped in front of my house when I fling the door open and jump out of the car. I rush to Fender's house and knock on the door.

When he doesn't answer in two seconds, I knock again.

The door flies open. "Quiet."

Oh no, he didn't. He did not tell me to quiet down. No one tells me to quiet down. Not anymore.

"You're not the boss of me," I hiss at him.

He points to the sofa where Isla's sleeping.

Shit. "Sorry."

I walk to the sofa and bend to pick my daughter up, but Fender nudges me out of the way. "I got this."

He gathers Isla in his arms and marches to the front door. I inhale a deep breath to stop myself from crying. All I've ever wanted is for Isla to have a father. A father who loves her. A father who carries her to bed when she falls asleep in front of the television.

I realize Fender is already halfway to my house and force my feet to move. I rush in front of him and unlock the door before motioning him inside.

"Bedroom," he rumbles.

I lead him toward Isla's room and he places her on the bed. She curls up on her side, fast asleep. She didn't notice me coming home or Fender carrying her. When my girl's out, she's out.

I kiss her forehead before following Fender to the front door.

"Thanks for watching my girl today."

He scowls. "Someone had to since all you do is work."

I rear back. "Excuse me?"

"You heard me. You work too much."

He turns and begins walking back to his house. I shut the door behind me and rush after him.

"Not so fast, mister. Who the hell do you think you are?"

"I'm the man who cared for your child for the past six hours. Where were you? Oh wait. I know. Working."

My nostrils flare. How dare he?

"You hardly talk and this is how you decide to break your silence? By being a complete and utter asshole?"

He crosses his arms over his chest. "Classic. You blame someone else since you can't accept responsibility for your daughter's welfare."

"I accept responsibility for my daughter's welfare." I pound my chest. "I'm the one who's been there since day one. I'm the one who's raised her on my own. It damn well wasn't her father who took off before she was six months old because 'babies are hard'. Or my parents who kicked me out when they found out I was pregnant. Never mind I was seventeen years old and a senior in high school."

"You should work less."

My word. He's like a dog with a bone. Good thing I grew up with a Great Dane. I got this.

I stab his chest with my finger. "I work as much as I can to give my daughter everything she wants. How do you think we can afford this house? It's not because my parents gave me any money or Isla's dad chipped in. No, this is all my hard work. I will work my fingers to the bone if it means Isla never has to suffer the way I did."

I realize I'm still touching his chest. In fact, my finger stabbing him has become my hand caressing him. Those muscles feel hard and strong. Strong enough to carry the burdens of the world.

What am I thinking? I yank my hand away.

"What Isla needs is a parent who's there for her."

Oh, no he didn't. He did not presume to know what's best for my daughter. I feel a muscle tick in my jaw. I wouldn't be surprised if steam is coming out of my ears.

"Are you saying I'm not there for my daughter?"

He opens his mouth but I slice a hand in the air. I'm talking now.

"I was there when she was teething. I was there when she had colic and screamed all night. I was there when she had explosive diarrhea and our entire apartment smelled rancid. I was there when she had nightmares after my grandparents died."

"You've made your point," he grumbles.

"I'm not done yet." I'm on a roll now. "I was there when she graduated from kindergarten. I was there when she got an award for learning her ABCs the fastest of everyone in the class. I was there when she did the citywide track meet and won a bronze medal for the high jump."

"Those things are all in the past. What about now?"

I consider his neck. It's big but I bet I could strangle him. Who's going to stop me? No one, that's who. I am a mother on a mission.

"It's a new job. I've only been in town for a few months. I need to settle in and train Brody. I've never been a personal assistant before. I need to show him I can do the job. Prove to him hiring me wasn't a mistake even though I have zero experience.

And I can't lose this job. I can't afford this house without it. And what kind of job can I get in Winter Falls if he fires me? The town isn't exactly teeming with businesses searching for managers."

Hold on. Why am I explaining myself to him?

"You know what. Never mind. From now on, I'll make sure Isla doesn't bother you."

I begin stomping toward my house.

"I like Isla."

The implication is clear. My daughter he likes. Me? Not so much. Yeah. Yeah. Mr. Grumpy Rockstar I got it already. The stay away vibes couldn't have been more obvious.

"She's very likable," I holler and keep moving.

"She's welcome at my house anytime."

Has he lost his dang mind? I whirl around on him.

"You seriously think I will allow my daughter to hang around a man who hates me?"

"I don't hate you."

"Who thinks I'm a bad parent?"

"Maybe I was—

"I can't believe I actually took the time to get you a present as a thank you," I mumble as I dig in my purse. I find the package and throw it at him. He catches it. Of course, he does. He can't fumble and look like a fool for one minute? Give me one second of glory? Is it too much to ask?

"What's this?"

"What do you think? The packaging isn't some elaborate surprise. Beef jerky."

"Beef jerky?"

I roll my eyes. "You can't buy beef jerky in Winter Falls. Something about the packaging being bad for the environment. I don't know. I thought you'd enjoy it since you're eating all the time. You don't want it? Give it back to me."

I hold out my hand but he retreats a step.

"Thank you."

"Whatever."

"I'll see you around."

Not if I see him first. I wasn't kidding. I'm done with the grumpy neighbor. I don't care how much Isla likes him. Or how sexy he is. Or how much I long to touch his naked body. Or how often I wake up sweaty in the middle of the night from dreaming of him.

I will not put up with a man who criticizes my life choices. Not anymore.

Chapter 8

Regret – To feel like shit because you're an idiot with a big mouth

FENDER

"Are you listening, grumpapottamus?" Gibson asks.

"Not grumpapottamus," I grumble.

Jett bursts into laughter. "Your grumbling proved us wrong. You're not grumpy at all."

Gibson leans close to whisper to me, "In case you're wondering, he's being sarcastic."

I push him away. "I'm not dumb."

"Didn't say you were. Socially inept? Maybe."

I frown. Does he have a point? After Leia let me have it last night, I realized I'm probably being a bit unfair to her. Okay fine. I am being unfair. I allowed my past to color my opinion of her. It's a shitty thing to do. I need to rectify this situation. But how?

Jett sighs. "He's daydreaming again."

I growl.

He clutches his chest. "Oh no. Grumpapottamus is growling at me. I'm scared."

"I'll save you." Gibson jumps to his feet and pretends to brandish a sword. "I'm the grumpapottamus slayer."

Jett grins. "You should get an outfit. You can put the initials GS on it for grumpapottamus slayer."

I swear if they refer to me as grumpapottamus one more time I will show them how grumpy I can be.

"Will you three pay attention?" Cash asks.

I grunt. I'm not the one causing a distraction.

He wags his finger at me. "Don't pretend you're innocent. You've been staring off into the distance since this meeting began."

"He's dreaming about Leia," Jett claims.

Gibson drops his head back and begins to pant. "Yes, Leia. Right there, Leia. Squeeze me harder."

My hand is around his neck before I realize I've moved. "Knock it off."

Gibson pulls at my hand but I don't let him go. "Say you'll stop."

Dylan sighs. "He can't talk when you're choking him."

I release the pressure on his neck a tiny bit. "Now say you'll stop."

"I'll stop," he chokes out and I release him.

"Water. I need water."

Dylan slides a glass toward him. "No more choking."

I make no promises. If Gibson sullies Leia's name again, I'll do what I have to.

Leia's had it tough enough. She doesn't need a bunch of idiot musicians making her life more difficult. My stomach twinges with guilt. I was the one making her life more difficult.

No more. From now on, I'll treat Leia with the respect she deserves. After hearing how difficult she's had it – how dare her asshole parents kick her out when she was seventeen and pregnant! – I'm going to make certain she gets no more trouble from me.

Cash throws a pencil at me. "No more choking and pay attention."

Jett snickers. "Fender's in trouble."

Cash pounds his fist on the table. "E-fucking-nough. This meeting is going to last forever if everyone doesn't calm down and pay attention."

"Is someone missing his sweetie?" Jett makes kissy faces.

Cash starts to stand but Dylan shackles his wrist to stop him. "He's trying to rile you up."

"Mission accomplished," Cash mutters as he sits down. "This meeting is never going to end."

"Not all of us have girlfriends at home," Jett says. "We're bored."

"But we don't want girlfriends to help out boredom," Gibson adds.

Jett rolls his eyes. "Of course not. This is established. No reason to reiterate."

Gibson shivers. "Since the big guy who claimed he would never want a relationship again is falling for Leia, I feel it's important to repeat our stance."

Jett nods. "Good point."

"As much as I'm enjoying how uncomfortable Fender is with this subject," Dylan begins and I realize I'm squirming in my seat.

Fuck. No wonder these assholes are making fun of me. They're sharks and they smell blood.

"I have a lunch date with my beautiful Ginny and I don't want to be late." The happiness on Dylan's face is clear. I thought I was happy with a woman once. I was wrong.

Gibson smirks. "Virginia is pretty."

Jett catches my eye. "I prefer blondes."

"Keep your dirty hands off Leia," I order him.

Cash chuckles. "Welcome to the jungle."

I am not in the jungle. I'm not anywhere near the jungle. Realizing I've been an ass to Leia doesn't automatically mean I'm ready to jump into bed with her. My pants tighten at the thought of Leia laid out for me in my bed.

Not ready to jump into bed with her, I remind my cock. He pouts as he deflates. He can pout all he wants. It's my hand or a one-night stand on offer to him. Nothing and no one else.

"Tour schedule," I grumble since someone has to get these yahoos back on track.

Cash taps the schedule with his pencil. "Did everyone get a chance to review the schedule Aurora sent?"

Jett purses his lips the same way he does every time our personal assistant's name is mentioned. He has it bad for the woman but refuses to get involved with her. He doesn't want a relationship with any woman. Ever.

"I bet Jett opened the email from Aurora before anyone else did," Gibson teases, proving he's a complete idiot.

Jett launches himself across the table at Gibson. I step out of the way as Dylan rushes to stop Jett.

"Enough!" Dylan shoves Jett off of Gibson and Jett falls to the floor. "Sit your asses down in your chairs now."

"Daddy's mad," Gibson mumbles but Dylan spears him with a glare and he snaps his mouth shut.

It's hard to ruffle Dylan but he has his limits and apparently his limit has been reached.

"Do I need to handcuff you to the chair or are you going to behave?" he asks Jett.

"I'm good." Jett slinks back to his chair and sits down.

"Finally," Cash begins once everyone is seated. "This schedule doesn't work for me."

"Or me," Dylan adds.

"I promised Indy I wouldn't be away from home for more than a week at a time," Cash explains.

"At least Indy can join us when it's summer vacation and she's off from school, Ginny can't since she's the librarian," Dylan complains.

"Will we depart from Winter Falls every time we have a tour stop?" Gibson asks.

"It seems unfair. We have to get our asses over to Colorado because the two of you fell in love." Jett's face practically turns green at the words 'fell in love'.

"You can always stay in Winter Falls," Cash reminds him.

"The lease on the house isn't up for several months," Dylan adds.

Cash motions to me. "Big guy isn't going anywhere."

"Because Leia's here," Gibson sings.

I glare at him. "You know why I'm not leaving."

He sobers. "Sorry, big guy."

The entire band knows my sad story. There aren't many secrets between the five of us. It's hard to keep a secret when you're on the road together for months at a time.

I wave away Gibson's apology.

"We can ask Aurora to handle travel arrangements for you two from wherever you are to the next concert stop, but you'll need to keep her appraised of your locations," Cash says.

"Yeah," Dylan agrees. "No slinking off to go rappelling off the Badlands Wall in the middle of the night."

"How else do you suggest I observe the stars at night in the Badlands?" Jett asks.

"With a telescope," Cash suggests.

"From the safety of a car," Dylan adds.

Jett sniffs. "Sounds boring."

Jett's search for adventure is going to get him killed if he doesn't slow down. Since he's busy running as fast as he can from his past, I don't expect him to slow down anytime soon.

"What if I don't know where I'll be?" Gibson asks.

I rub a hand down my face. Gibson is a heavy drinker who thinks charming women out of their panties should be an Olympic sport. He refuses to be tied down to a schedule because he wants to be able to follow a different woman to bed every night.

Cash shrugs. "You can make your way to the venue on your own."

Gibson's nose wrinkles. "Arrange my own travel? That's what Aurora's for."

Jett growls. "Aurora isn't your personal assistant."

"But you want her to be *your* personal assistant." Gibson waggles his eyebrows.

Here we go again. My stomach rumbles to remind me it's been several hours since breakfast. I stand.

"Hungry."

"The brewery's open. I could go for a burger," Jett says.

"And one of their new IPAs," Gibson adds.

I frown. Gibson's been drinking way too much lately. I've tried hiding his beer but he always finds it or buys more. He can't manage to buy groceries – he's always stealing mine – but beer, he's never without.

"I'm off to meet Ginny. I'll meet you guys back here in an hour," Dylan says and hurries out the door without a backward glance.

"You coming?" Jett asks Cash as we walk toward the door.

Cash sighs. "I better before you manage to get yourself banned from *Naked Falls Brewery.*"

Gibson snorts. "Don't be silly. The brewery's owned by two of your brothers. We won't get banned."

I follow them out of the recording studio. I notice Isla playing around with some kids across the street at the Community

Center and wave to her. She waves back. Good. She must not have heard the knock-down drag-out fight I had with her mom in their front yard last night.

I rub a hand over my chest as guilt swarms me. I need to fix what I screwed up with Leia. But I don't know how. I don't exactly have a good track record with women.

Chapter 9

Meatloaf – An excuse to bring two people together

FENDER

The bell over the door at *Moon's Diner* chimes as I walk in. I scan the restaurant. There's not a table free. Not surprising since it's meatloaf night, which is why I'm here. This place has the best homemade meatloaf I've ever eaten.

I make my way to the counter and sit there.

"Hey, Fender," Moon, the owner of the diner, stops in front of me. "You want the usual?"

I grunt.

She makes a checkmark in the air. "Check! Another exciting conversation with Fender Hays."

I grunt again.

She giggles. "If I found grumpy men sexy, I would chase after you until you gave up from exhaustion."

"But you're engaged," a man I assume is her fiancé hollers across the room.

"We agreed I can flirt with other men."

"No, you proclaimed you can flirt with other men, Moonbeam."

"I'm not understanding the difference."

A pang of envy hits me at their easy bantering. I want what they have. I thought I had it once, but it was all a lie.

Moon sighs. "Do you see what I have to put up with?"

"Will you stop your bickering and get my food?" the old man next to me asks.

She rolls her eyes. "Of course, Old Man Mercury. Coming right up." She twirls away.

"They're up to no good," he says once she's gone.

I glance around but there isn't anyone else sitting at the counter.

"I'm speaking to you, Fender Hays."

"Do I know you?"

"I'm Mercury, one of the founders of Winter Falls."

I lift my hand to shake his but he scowls at me and I drop my hand. "Nice to meet you."

"Liar."

I chuckle. He called my bluff. This old guy is cool.

"Who's up to something?" I ask.

"The old ladies of this town."

"The gossip gals?" The gossip gals are a hoot.

"They do enjoy their gossip."

I don't disagree with him. There's a reason the ladies dubbed themselves the gossip gals after all.

"They're interfering where they shouldn't be."

"What do you mean?"

Before he can answer, Moon arrives with two carry-out bags. "Here you go."

I'm confused. "I didn't order takeout. I was planning to eat here. And this is a lot of food." Even for me.

"And now she claims she's out of meatloaf," someone hollers from behind me.

Moon sticks her tongue out at him. "These meals were ordered in advance."

My brow wrinkles. "In advance? I didn't order in advance."

"I have it written down." She opens her notepad and reads, "Two meatloaf meals for Fender and Leia."

"Leia? I didn't order food for Leia."

"Nonetheless." She taps the bags. "Better deliver it to her before it gets cold."

I glance over at Mercury to ask him if this is what he meant about the gossip gals being up to something but he's disappeared.

The bell behind her rings. "Food's up!"

"I'll put it on your tab," she says as she scurries away.

This is ridiculous. I was planning to eat here. Not at home where my roommates can steal my food. And I didn't order a meal for Leia. Why would I order food for the woman who hates me?

Hold on. I can deliver this to Leia as a kind gesture. It won't make up for what an ass I've been but it can't hurt. Good plan. I smirk as I pick up the bags and make my way to the exit of the diner.

I can smell the meatloaf and potatoes as I walk up Leia's porch steps and knock on the door. My stomach rumbles in anticipation.

"Good. You're back," she says as she swings the door open. She scowls when she realizes it's me. "You're not Indigo."

I lift the bag. "I brought your order from the diner."

Her brow wrinkles. "My order from the diner? What is going on today? First, Indigo shows up and steals my daughter. And then you show up with food I didn't order."

"You didn't order this food?"

She snorts. "I didn't even know it was possible to get takeout from the diner. Isn't takeout bad for the environment?"

"I have an arrangement with the diner."

"Must be nice to be a rockstar," she grumbles.

She has no idea. Being a rockstar isn't all it's made out to be. Why else are all five of us hiding out in the small town of Winter Falls where no one cares who we are, fans are unceremoniously kicked out of town, and the paparazzi are practically banned?

"Do you want the food?"

"Are you kidding? I'm drooling from the smell alone. Moon is crazy but she knows how to cook."

I hand her the bag and she frowns. "This is heavy."

"The only way Moon would agree to give me takeout is if I accept the food on normal plates with proper silverware and promise to return it all the next day."

I hesitate for a moment. I need to apologize for how I behaved.

"Can we talk?"

She sighs before motioning me inside. "I'm not waiting any longer to eat this food. And you better not ruin my appetite with some bullshit about how I'm a horrible mother. I have a baseball bat and I know how to use it."

I clear my throat to stop myself from laughing at her threat. She's growling at me, but all I can think about is how adorable she is.

She leads me to the small dining table off of the kitchen. I scan her home and notice it's dated but clean and tidy. The walls and carpets are beige but the pillows and blankets add pops of color and there are pictures on the wall. This place has a personality.

I wait for her to sit down before sitting across from her. She opens her bag and the smell of meatloaf and potatoes escapes. My stomach growls.

She motions to my bag. "Go ahead. You might as well eat before it gets cold." She pauses. "Or do you want to say I'm an unfit mother again? In which case, let me grab my rolling pin."

I swallow my laughter since I don't think she's kidding about the rolling pin. "No. Actually, I need to apologize."

Her mouth drops open. "Apologize? You are going to apologize to me?"

"Um, yeah."

"This ought to be good. A man's never apologized to me before."

"Never?"

She shakes her head. "Nope."

"Not even Isla's dad when he left you?"

She barks out a laugh. "You're funny. I never knew you were funny."

"I'm not being funny."

"If you knew, you'd understand."

"Knew what?"

She wipes tears of mirth from her eyes. "How Charles packed his things in the middle of the night while I was passed out from days of not sleeping since Isla had colic. How my lawyers could never find him to sue him for child support. How I haven't heard from him in eleven years."

"Isla's dad doesn't pay child support?"

She rolls her eyes. "Why do you think I work my ass off? This house doesn't pay for itself."

And I was the asshole who yelled at her for working too hard.

"Sorry I said you should work less."

She holds up a hand. "Okay. You need to stop saying the words sorry and apologize. My heart can't handle this many surprises in one day."

"And I'm sorry I said you weren't a good mother."

She narrows her eyes. "You're trying to kill me, aren't you?"

"You're a good mom."

She clutches her chest. "Oh no. You did it. I'm a goner."

She gasps as she falls out of her chair onto the floor. I stand above her to observe the performance.

Her eyes pop open. "What do you think? Worth a standing ovation?"

"You'll have to do better. I live with Gibson and Jett remember?"

I hold out my hand to help her stand. As soon as my hand touches her, a jolt of warmth hits me and travels from my hand through my body down to my groin.

Guessing by how Leia's mouth is gaping open, she's feeling it, too.

I rub circles with my thumb on her hand. Her skin's as soft as I thought it would be. I wonder how soft those lips are. How would they feel against mine? I lean closer intent on finding out.

Leia yanks her hand from mine and shoves me away. "No."

I immediately retreat. When a woman says no, I listen. "Why no?"

"I'm not a one-night stand kind of girl."

I knew she wasn't. But when I touched her soft skin, I lost my mind and forgot.

"One night is all I can offer." I begin packing up my food. "I'll finish this at home."

"Good idea." She shows me to the door.

I pause on her porch. "I meant what I said. I am sorry for being a jerk."

"Thank you for your apology."

Thank you is not acceptance. But what did I think? I could apologize and everything would be fine between us? I've been a complete asshole to her. She has no reason to believe I'm not always an asshole.

I'll have to prove to her with my actions I'm more than the asshole I've shown her over the past weeks.

Chapter 10

Doubt – When temptation begins to override your good sense

LEIA

Isla stomps her foot and whines, "Mom!"

"No."

"I want him to come with."

But I don't. Fender may be a sweetheart to her. To me? He's not so nice.

But he did bring you food and apologize.

I ignore my inner voice.

And he's pretty to look at.

Apparently, my inner voice doesn't remember how Fender told me I'm a bad mom and how I work too much.

"I bet Fender's ridden a horse before. We should probably have someone with us who knows how to ride a horse."

I groan. This is what I get for giving in to my daughter. I told her I'd maybe get her a pony ride for her birthday and what happens? Her birthday is still five months off and here we are going to ride a pony.

"Brody said I could invite one friend."

I sigh. Damn Brody. He overheard me arguing with Isla about a pony ride and the next thing I know, I'm getting a bonus in the form of a coupon for three people to attend a trail ride.

"Why don't you ask one of your friends from the community center?"

She crosses her arms over her chest. "I want Fender."

Crap. Her face screams stubborn. She's not giving up until she gets what she wants. I make one last ditch effort.

"Fender's a busy man. You can't expect him to drop everything to spend the day with us."

She shrugs. "Let's go ask him."

She doesn't wait for me but barges out of the house and races across the yard to next door. And here I was really excited about this house. No one warned me a sexy rockstar would move in next door.

No, not sexy. Fender isn't sexy.

He's sex on a stick and you know it.

Oh, shut up.

By the time I catch up to Isla, she's already pounding on the door. "Fender! Fender! Fender!"

I check the time and realize it's barely nine a.m. What time do rockstars wake up?

"Honey, he's probably still asleep."

My hopes are dashed when the door opens and Fender appears. His hair is wet. Was he in the shower? Was he naked in the shower? Oh boy. I can imagine how sexy those muscles of his are when he's all wet with water pouring down on him.

"Fender!" Isla screams and jumps into his arms.

Fender smiles at her and his face transforms from grumpity grump to sexy boy next door with a body made for sin.

"Good morning, Isla," he greets. "What's going on?" he asks as he sets her down.

"We're going on a pony ride!"

"Keep it down, Isla. Fender's roommates might still be sleeping."

"Too late," Jett grumbles. His hair is all disheveled and his eyes are red-rimmed. "What time is it?" he asks as he scratches his jaw.

"Time for a pony ride!" Isla yells.

Jett chuckles. "Good thing Gibson didn't come home last night. Waking him up early is not a good idea."

My brow wrinkles. "Gibson didn't come home last night? Is he okay? He's not lying dead or injured in a ditch somewhere, is he?"

He shrugs. "I have no idea where he is."

"Don't you keep tabs on each other to make sure no one gets in trouble? Or hurt?"

Fender glares at me. "Gibson's fine."

"If he's not, I'm holding you responsible."

He ignores me to ask Isla, "What's this about a pony ride?"

"I've always wanted a horse but Mom says they're too much work."

"We're going on a trail ride," I explain as Isla's answer wasn't much of an answer. "My boss gave it to me as a bonus for all my hard work."

"Good." He nods. "You deserve it."

I deserve it? Is Fender feeling okay? Does he have a fever? Is this the same man who yelled at me several times for how much I work?

He also apologized.

I blow out a breath. Fine. I won't attack him for being a hypocrite no matter how much fun it would be.

"And I can bring a friend!" Isla exclaims.

"I'm the friend, aren't I?" Jett asks. "I'll get my riding gear on."

"He has riding gear?" I ask.

Fender frowns. "Don't ask."

Isla tugs on Fender's jeans to get his attention. "You're my friend. I want you to come with."

"Me?" Fender asks.

"Don't you want to come?" She thrusts out her bottom lip in a pout. She's pulling out the big guns.

"I'd love to join you."

Darn. There goes my chance of avoiding him for the day.

"We'll leave as soon as I return from the city hall with the car." Since Winter Falls is anti-car due to their whole environmental thing, there are cars locals can borrow whenever they need to travel further than the town's limits.

"Don't bother. We can use Cash's."

"I'm ready," Jett announces as he rushes toward us.

I bite my bottom lip. I only have tickets for three of us to do the trail ride. I guess I can use some of the money in my emergency fund to pay for him.

"Don't worry. Tweedle Dum will pay for himself."

I narrow my eyes on Fender. How did he know what I was thinking? He smiles in return. A real one with those dimples on display. I quickly look away. Those dimples are lethal.

"I guess we're ready."

Isla jumps in the air. "Yee-haw!"

I ruffle her hair. I will not be the type of mom to shoot her down when she's having fun no matter how loud or silly she is. In other words, I will not be my mom.

The horse ranch where we're doing the trail ride is a thirty-minute drive. It's not a silent journey. Not when my daughter's around. Jett and Isla sit in the backseat and she jabbers to him the entire way.

When we arrive, I expect Jett to rush out of the car to escape my little chatterbox. But he helps Isla out of the car with a smile on his face. My girl can charm anyone. Fender pushes Jett out of the way to grasp Isla's hand – even the King of Grumps.

"Hi!" a woman greets. "I'm Tammy. And you must be Leia and Isla." Her gaze catches on Fender and her eyes flare. "And who might these gentlemen be?"

My stomach cramps and my hands tighten into fists. Who does this hussy think she is? Hitting on Fender while he's standing next to me holding my daughter's hand.

Whoa. I sound jealous. Shit. I am jealous. I force my hands to relax. I refuse to be jealous with regard to Fender. He's not mine to be jealous of.

"I'm Jett. I'm the experienced one of the bunch." He waggles his eyes to make it clear he's not referring to experience with a horse.

Tammy rakes her gaze over him. Her eyes widen and her mouth drops open. I'm surprised she doesn't lick her lips.

"I have some experience with horses," Fender adds.

Tammy kneels in front of Isla. "What about you? Any experience?" Isla shakes her head.

"Mom neither," I add.

"Not a problem." Tammy motions us toward the stables. "We'll get you kitted out."

Jett snags Isla and puts her on his shoulders. "I'll help the little one." He pretends to gallop away before I have a chance to protest.

We reach the stables and Tammy gives us some tips before showing us to our horses.

"Umm…" This thing – no, not thing, Patty is her name. Patty's huge. I don't know how I'm supposed to get on her, let alone ride her.

"Shall I help you?" Fender asks from way too close behind me. I can feel his breath on my neck. Goosebumps arise and I lock my muscles down tight before I shiver.

"T-t-thank you," I stutter.

"I'm going to touch you now."

He steps closer until I feel his body surrounding me. His musky scent wraps around me. I can imagine how it would feel to be in his arms. I bet I would feel safe and protected. My knees go weak and I wobble.

"Easy. No reason to be scared."

Scared of being with him? I'm not scared. I'm excited. My panties are damp just thinking about it. I bet he's a considerate lover. I bet he wouldn't come first before rolling off me and starting to snore while his pants are still around his ankles.

"You got this," he murmurs as he places his hands on my hips and lifts me up to straddle the horse.

Oh my, he's strong. His muscles didn't strain to lift me.

"You're strong." The words are out before I can stop them. "And big."

I can see he's big. He winks.

Oh, he's not referring to his complete body. He's referring to one particular body part. A body part I wouldn't mind touching with my hands and mouth. And being filled with. Too bad he only wants a one-night stand with me.

But can't we take him for a ride anyway? It's been a long time.

It has. My eyes are glued to his body as he mounts his horse. Strong and agile. Maybe I should make an exception to my no one-night stands rule.

Chapter 11

Epiphany – The moment you realize you've been blind to the possibility in front of you

FENDER

I play the final notes of the song, and the sound reverberates throughout the venue until silence falls. The silence lasts for a millisecond before the crowd erupts in cheers. Finally, we're done. Not only with this concert but with the week of back-to-back concerts.

I set my bass down before exiting the stage. Jett, Gibson, Dylan, and Cash follow me.

"Encore! Encore! Encore!"

I ignore the crowd. I've heard concert-goers yell for *Cash & the Sinners* to perform an encore for years now. It no longer excites me.

I scowl. It no longer excites me? Since when? On our tour last year, I was pumped whenever I came off stage. Full of restless energy and excitement. Why not now?

"Dude." Jett elbows me. "Get with the program."

"He's not dude. He's grumpapottamus," Gibson says.

"Are you okay?" Dylan asks. "We're about to go back on."

I grunt. I'm perfectly fine. Why do they think something's wrong?

"He's grunting. He's fine," Cash says.

Dylan rolls his eyes. "You're just saying he's fine because you want to get this encore done and get back home."

Cash chuckles. "Don't act as if you're not in a hurry to get home, too."

Dylan shrugs. "It's only been a week, but this week has lasted forever."

Jett rears back. "Forever? This week has been awesome."

"I second," Gibson says. "Awesome week."

"Because you took those twins back to your hotel room the other night."

Gibson grins. "Hell, yeah. Do you think there's an app for finding twins? I'm all over it."

Dylan rolls his eyes. "You're disgusting is what you are."

Gibson smirks. "What I am is winning."

Jett scowls. "Twins don't count as two women."

Gibson waggles his eyebrows. "They certainly do. Ask me how many condoms I used."

I growl. I don't want to listen to this shit. It's bad enough when we're on the tour bus and can't get away from the details, which he exaggerates to absurdity. "Encore."

"Everyone ready?" Cash asks. Despite his desire to hurry back home, there's still a sparkle of excitement in his eyes. He loves performing before a crowd.

He waits for everyone to nod. "Let's go!" He claps.

Jett rushes on stage first. He begins to drum out a beat and Gibson joins him with his rhythm guitar. I'm next. I strum my bass as Dylan strolls on stage before Cash finally makes an appearance.

When Cash appears, the crowd goes wild. Our manager was worried that his being in a steady relationship with Indigo would have a negative effect on our fans, but the fans adore him now more than ever. According to the press, 'there's nothing sexier than a man committed to his woman'.

We play three songs before Cash signals for us to wrap it up. Good. I'm ready to get home.

Home? Winter Falls isn't home. No matter how much I enjoy living there. It's not permanent. It's temporary until I find a place to settle down.

But another place won't have Leia and Isla in it. I pat the card in my back pocket. I glance around backstage to be certain I'm alone before pulling it out again.

The picture on the front is of a doggy with big puppy dog eyes and the words *We'll miss you when you're gone* underneath him.

I open it. Inside, Isla wrote me a note. *Come back soon. Hugs, Isla.*

My heart warms as I stare at her wobbly block letters. Too bad Leia didn't add her name to the card.

Leia. I've missed her this past week. I've missed my little firecracker. I've missed how soft her skin is. How she shivers when I speak close to her ear. How her knees wobble when I surround her.

She thinks I didn't notice her response to me at the horse farm. I miss nothing where she's concerned. Including how she shut off her reaction to me.

I know she wants me. But she doesn't want to get involved with me. Is it because I was an asshole? I can show her I'm not.

I freeze. What the hell am I thinking? Am I seriously contemplating a relationship with Leia? I don't do relationships. Not after how the last one ended.

"What's this?" Jett nabs the card from me.

I growl and start after him. He throws the card to Gibson who sprints down the hallway. I chase after him but Jett blocks my way. I push him to the side and continue after Gibson.

"Private," I grumble and snatch my card back.

"But it's from Isla. She's our friend, too," Gibson says.

"I even let her win at tag." Jett never lets anyone win. He's the most competitive person I've ever met.

"She's a little girl," I remind him. She's not competition.

"Still," he pouts.

"What's going on?" Cash asks as he enters the hallway. "Why is security complaining about you playing catch in the hallway?"

I narrow my eyes at Jett. "Not playing catch."

He holds up his hands. "It's not as if I stole a love letter from Leia to you. It was a card from Isla."

"A card given *to* me."

"Why is Isla giving cards to this asshole and not us?" Gibson asks.

"Isla? Leia's daughter?" Dylan asks as he joins us. His face is flushed and there's a twinkle in his eye. He must have been on the phone with Virginia.

Jett points at Dylan's face. "Someone was having phone sex with his girlfriend again."

"I never thought the shy librarian would be into phone sex," Gibson says.

Dylan glares at him. "No more talk of Ginny and sex."

Gibson curls his bottom lip in a pout. "But I want all the details. I tell you all the details of my exploits."

"Ginny is not an exploit. She's the woman I love."

I wait for the pang of jealousy to hit me the way it always does whenever Dylan or Cash refer to the women they love but it doesn't come. Instead of jealousy, all I feel is longing.

Longing to be with Leia and Isla now instead of standing in this hallway with my bandmates waiting to go home. I want Leia in my arms where she belongs.

Where she belongs? Fuck. I rub a hand down my face. I want Leia.

I knew I wanted her the first second I saw her. How could I not with her mischievous blue eyes and curly blonde hair?

But I swore off relationships after what *she* did to me. I never wanted to open myself up to another person again. Never wanted to feel the pain of having everything I've ever wanted ripped away from me again.

But with Leia, I'm not worried about opening myself. I'm not panicked. Quite the opposite.

Imagining the little firecracker as mine has excitement coursing through me. I'm ready to take a chance again with Leia.

Chapter 12

Distraction – A ruse to prevent the gossip gals from concentrating on your love life

LEIA

I trudge up the courtroom steps. I'm tired and in no mood to attend a Winter Falls business meeting. But Brody insisted I attend on his behalf tonight, so here I am.

"Oh good, you're here," Sage says when I enter the building.

And she's not alone. All of the gossip gals are with her. And the gleams in their eyes say they are up to something. I have a feeling these ladies are always up to something. Whoever said small town living is boring hasn't met the gossip gals.

"Good evening. Sorry, I can't stay to chat. I need to get to a meeting." I indicate the meeting room.

"As do we," Feather says.

I glance around the group and notice they're all nodding.

"I thought this was a business meeting."

Clove frowns. "And we're all businesswomen. I own *Clove's Coffee Corner*."

"And *Sensual Scents* is mine," Petal adds.

"I own *Feather's Frozen Delights*," Feather says.

"I used to own the yoga studio, *Earth Bliss,* but I recently retired."

Recently? Cayenne can't be a day under eighty and she was recently managing a yoga studio? Meanwhile, I can barely touch my toes.

"I technically don't have a business, but I basically run this town," Sage claims.

I cross my arms over my chest and raise my eyebrows. "You run this town?"

Feather rubs her hands together. "I do love a spunky heroine."

Is she referring to me? I'm not a heroine in one of her romance novels.

"Indigo had spunk," Petal claims.

Clove points at me. "But this one's a firecracker."

Feather studies me. "If this were a book, she'd have red hair."

"Ladies," I cut them off, "as much as I'm enjoying your compliments, I do need to get to the meeting. Brody's orders."

I salute them and march away without looking back.

The meeting room is packed when I enter. Considering the size of Winter Falls, I'd assumed there'd be ten attendants, twenty tops. Another reminder to never assume.

Indigo waves me over. She's sitting with Virginia at the front of the room.

"What are you two doing here?" I ask when I join them.

Virginia frowns. "I'm here under protest."

"My grandmother told me all about the town business meetings. I wasn't going to miss one." Indigo is practically bouncing in her seat.

"And guess who got dragged along?" Virginia mumbles.

"I'm only here because Brody insisted. He wants to check there are no problems with his plans to build a swimming pool."

I don't know what I'm supposed to do if there are problems. I know nothing about permits or plans for swimming pools.

"Here." Indigo shoves a beer into my hands.

"I'm at work," I hiss and try to give it back to her. "I shouldn't be drinking."

"Why not? Everyone else is." She motions around the room.

She's not lying. Several people are drinking beer and eating popcorn. In fact, there's a drink cart set up in the back of the room with a long line of people waiting to buy beer and popcorn.

"Did you at least buy some popcorn?" I ask.

Indigo grins and points to the bucket on the seat next to her.

"At least this is better than sitting at home wondering what Dylan's up to," Virginia mutters.

Dylan and the rest of the *Cash & the Sinners* band are doing a short one-week tour on the West Coast to launch their latest single.

"Are you worried?"

Virginia scrunches up her nose. "No?"

Indigo throws an arm around her shoulders. "She's not worried because being worried would be silly. Dylan loves you very much. He wouldn't risk what you two have together by being stupid. Besides, when does he have time to be stupid? He phones you as soon as each concert is over."

She waggles her eyebrows making it obvious what the two get up to on the phone. Virginia blushes. Huh. I wouldn't expect the shy librarian to have phone sex with a rockstar but what do I know? The extent of my sexual encounters could fit onto a postcard.

Indigo elbows me. "What about you? Missing Fender?"

I scowl at her. "Miss how annoying my neighbor is? Nope. I'm good."

"I heard he wasn't annoying on the trail ride. Quite the opposite." She winks.

Memories of Fender touching me as he helped me to mount my horse assault me. How his breath felt against my neck. How his hands felt on my hips. How his warmth surrounded me. How I thought of his naked body in the shower later that night.

I clear my throat and force those thoughts away before I get all hot and bothered at a business meeting in front of the whole town.

"I don't know what you're referring to."

Virginia and Indigo burst into laughter. Indigo points to my face. "Liar, liar, pants on fire."

I scowl at Virginia. "I thought you were on my side."

"I'm on the side of love."

"Love?" I scoff. "I can't stand the grumpapottamus."

"Which is why you have a cute pet name for him."

"Grumpapottamus is not a cute pet name."

Bang! Bang! Bang!

A woman hits a gavel against the table at the front of the room before announcing, "I now call the July business meeting to order."

I lean close to Indigo to ask, "Who's she?"

Virginia trembles. "Rain."

"What's with the trembling? Should I be scared of her? Is she the big bad witch?"

"You make fun but I think Rain is a fortune teller."

"A fortune teller? Does she have a crystal ball?"

Virginia narrows her eyes on me. "I'm serious."

I raise an eyebrow at Indigo and she fills me in, "Rain owns the jewelry store in town, *Bohemian Treasures.* She's also the mayor this year."

"The first order of business is the Lughnasadh festival next week," Rain announces.

"Disagree!" Sage hollers.

Rain sighs. "We agreed to discuss the town's business before you started with your matchmaking."

Matchmaking? Who are they trying to matchmake now? I scan the room but I have no idea who their target could be.

"But I want to know when Leia's going to let Fender butter her biscuit!" Feather shouts.

I jump to my feet. "I told you I don't want to be matched."

"We can't help what fate decides," Clove says.

Sage grins. "But we do enjoy helping fate along."

"Now answer the question," Feather insists.

"What question?"

"When are you going to let Fender butter your biscuit?"

"I don't know what that means."

"We read it in a book by Lyra Parish." Feather fans herself. "It was hot."

"Fender is not coming anywhere near my biscuit. Or my butter. Or anything of mine."

"But Isla loves him," Cayenne whines. Yes, an elderly woman with gray hair can whine.

"She also loves Barney but I won't be dating a purple dinosaur anytime soon."

Bang! Bang! Bang!

I force my attention to the front of the room but Rain isn't banging her gavel. An old man knocks his cane on the floor as he stands.

"Enough!" he growls.

"You're no fun, Mercury!" Petal shouts at him.

"You used to be fun," Sage adds.

"And you ladies used to have your own lives and not interfere in everyone else's."

Laughter erupts in the room.

"They did?"

"When was this?"

"I don't know."

"I don't believe this."

Guess I'm not the only one surprised by Mercury's words.

Indigo giggles. "I'm never missing another one of these meetings."

"Easy for you to say. You're not the target."

She shrugs. "You're handling them perfectly fine on your own."

Of course, I am. I can handle anything that comes my way. I'm a single mom. It's my superpower.

"Do you not like Fender?" Virginia asks.

"Let me count the ways I do not like Fender. One, he's a grump. Two, he thinks I'm a bad parent."

He apologized for saying those things.

I ignore my inner voice. She's not on my side tonight.

"Three, he thinks I'm a workaholic."

"And, four, he's sexy and you want to get in his pants," Indigo says.

I point to her beer bottle. "How many have you had of those?"

"One."

Virginia snorts. "Are you forgetting about the one you had with dinner?"

Indigo shrugs. "Who's counting?"

Virginia sighs. "Not you. Indigo and math are not friends."

"It's impossible to be friends with a school subject."

"Be nice, Mercury, or we'll put you in a home!" Sage yells and the entire room stills.

Mercury slowly turns to face Sage. "What did you say?"

"Someone's in trouble," Indigo sings next to me and I elbow her to be quiet.

I glance between Sage and Mercury. They both appear about to say words that can't be taken back. I know all about saying words that can't be taken back.

I jump to my feet. "I'm supposed to ask about the permit for the public pool. Is a pool bad for the environment?"

The word environment is barely out of my mouth before chaos erupts.

I pretend to polish my fingernails on my shirt. "My work here is done."

And no one is discussing matching me with Fender any longer. Win! Win!

You wouldn't mind letting Fender butter your biscuit.

Stupid inner voice. She hasn't been this much trouble since I was seventeen and she claimed not using a condom wouldn't be a big deal. She was wrong then and she's wrong now.

Fender Hays is not the grump for me. No way. No how.

Chapter 13

Determined – how you feel when the woman you want turns you down

FENDER

"Fender!" Isla screams. She barrels her way through the crowd at the Lughhasadh festival toward me.

I pick her up and twirl her around. "How are you, cutie pie?"

She throws her arms around my neck as she giggles. "We missed you."

We? I glance over at Leia who's scowling at us. She doesn't appear to have missed me the way I missed her.

I kiss Isla's cheek before setting her on the ground. I meet Leia's gaze as I say, "I missed you both, too."

Her scowl deepens. And I'm supposed to be the grumpy one.

"Come on, Isla. Fender has better things to do than hang out with us."

"No, I don't."

Leia opens her mouth but before she can give me a piece of her mind – and there's no doubt she's ready to give it to me – Sage hollers her name from across the street.

Leia glances toward the heavens. "You have got to be kidding me."

"How is our little girl today?" Feather asks as she approaches with the rest of the gossip gals trailing behind her. Except Sage, of course. She's vying with Feather to be at the front of the group. These ladies crack me up.

"Do you want to play carnival games with us?" Petal asks Isla.

"Carnival games?" Isla asks.

"Darts, ring toss, those kinds of things," Clove explains.

"We even have a whack-a-mole, except the mole is an oil rig," Cayenne says.

Isla tugs on Leia's sleeve. "Can I, Mom? Can I?"

Leia sighs. "Let me give you some money."

She reaches into her pocket but Sage stops her. "It's on us."

Feather holds out her hand. "Come on, Isla."

Isla grabs her hand and with a wave, she's gone.

"I should have known," Leia mutters as the gossip gals lead her daughter away.

"Known what?" I ask, although I don't think she intended for me to hear her.

She throws her arms in the air. "Apparently the gossip gals are matchmakers and guess who they've 'matched' me with?"

My brow wrinkles. What the hell? The gossip gals are matching Leia? "Who?"

She points to me. "You, grumpystiltskin."

I cough to hide my amusement at the situation. This is what the gossip gals are up to? Matching me with Leia? This is the best news I've heard in a while.

"Hmmm…." I pretend to consider the matter. "Maybe we should go out on a date."

She fast blinks. "What? Did you not understand what I said?"

Oh, I understood her. And I'm taking full advantage of the situation. This is the perfect opportunity to initiate my plan to make Leia mine.

"I understood," I grumble.

She crosses her arms over her chest and taps her foot. "And yet you asked me out? You might as well throw lighter fuel on the fire. Boom!" She mimics an explosion with her hands.

I shrug. "Maybe the date will be a disaster and then they'll leave us alone." It won't be. I'll make sure of it.

She snorts. "I don't know those women well, but I know they're not leaving us alone until we're either married or I'm pregnant."

The vision of Leia's stomach swollen with my baby pops into my mind. I wait for the panic to arise. It always does when I consider children after what *she* did. But there's no panic. I knew the decision to take a chance on Leia was the right one.

I shackle her wrist and draw her away from the crowd. She snarls at me but she doesn't kick and scream. Progress.

As soon as we're alone, she yanks her hand from my hold. "What the hell, Fender?"

"I need to explain some things to you."

"If it's about the birds and bees, there's no need. I kind of already figured it out. I present Exhibit 1 – my child."

I chuckle. "Not about the birds and the bees."

"Good. Those discussions are brutal. I think I have PTSD from when I explained it all to Isla." She shivers.

"No birds and bees talk."

"Okay. You dragged me here, grumpy caveman. What do you want to discuss?"

I brought Leia here fully intending to explain to her about my past. But now we're here, I don't know where to begin. I've never told anyone what happened before. I've never needed to tell anyone before. The band knows everything because they had front-row seats to the shit show.

I clear my throat. "Um."

She holds up her hand. "I get you want the gossip gals off your back but you don't have to ask me out."

"What if I want to ask you out?"

She rolls her eyes. "You've been sending out 'leave me alone' vibes since the minute we met."

"Not intentional."

"Really?"

I shrug. "I'm used to pushing people away. It's hard to change now."

"But you want to change?"

"Yes." I clear my throat. "Do you want to go out with me?"

She doesn't hesitate. "No."

"No?"

"Are you having hearing difficulties? No!" She rejects me loud enough for the entire town to hear.

"Why not?"

Her eyes widen. "You seriously have to ask?" I nod. "Okay. Let me count the ways. One, you think I'm a bad parent. Two, you think I work too much. And, three, I don't wanna."

Oh, she wants to. Her body doesn't lie. Her pupils are dilated as she heaves for breath while staring at my chest. But she's holding herself back.

"I apologized."

"And I thanked you for your apology but I did not accept it."

"Can I explain why I was an asshat?"

"Asshat? It's good you can recognize your own faults."

I smile. This woman is a firecracker.

She gasps. "No fair. You can't bring out the dimples when you ask me out. It gives you an unfair advantage."

My smile widens. "Unfair advantage?"

"You know what I mean."

I make sure both of my dimples are on display. "How about now? Will you go out on a date with me now?"

She crosses her arms over her chest. "What part of no are you not understanding? And why did you bring me to an alley to ask me out? Are you embarrassed of me?"

I rub a hand down my face. How did we go from 'my dimples are a weapon' to 'I'm embarrassed of her'? Women! I'll never understand them. But they are fascinating.

"I wanted to explain my past."

"You're serious. You're going to tell me about your past?" I nod and her eyes widen. "You're not worried I'll sell your story to some sleazy magazine?"

"Nope."

She taps her cheek. "I wonder what the going rate is for spilling the beans on Fender Hays' past is?"

"Do you want to know or not?"

"Oh, I want to know. I want to know everything. The more the better. Those rags pay by the word."

She's bluffing. She'd never sell my story.

"I trust you."

"You should. I'm a very reliable person. Hardworking, quick to pick up new tasks, not afraid to get my hands dirty."

"Are you reciting your resume to me?"

"Is it helping?"

"I said I trust you."

She motions with her hand. "By all means, begin with the spilling the beans portion of the day."

"I had a serious relationship once," I blurt out. "Her name was Vicki."

"Vicki with an 'I' I bet. She probably was a cheerleader."

"I met her backstage at one of our concerts. She was a fan."

"Half the world is a fan," she mutters.

"I took Vicki to the hotel room and we... ah... um..."

"Had sex," Leia fills in.

"Yes," I nod. "We had sex."

"I don't understand why you're telling me about having sex with another woman. Pro tip. If you're trying to convince a woman to go out on a date with you, don't lead with I had sex with fans."

"Let me finish," I grumble.

"There's the grumpy pants we know and love."

"Vicki got pregnant that night."

Her eyes widen to the size of saucers. "You have a kid? I rescind my decision not to sell your story to the tabloids. This is gold."

"I don't have a child."

Pain slices through me and I clutch my stomach before it spills out onto the road. Leia squeezes my hand.

"Shit. I'm sorry. I was joking. What happened? Did she lose the baby? I'm so sorry."

Pain turns to anger at the reminder of the truth of what happened with Vicki. I pause to let the anger coursing through my body dissipate before I continue. I'm not mad at Leia. It's not her fault. "She said she did."

Leia throws her arms around me and hugs me tightly. "Oh Fender."

I lay my cheek on the top of her head and breathe in her scent. Lemons. She smells of lemons. I love the clean scent of lemons. Now more than ever.

I enjoy the feel of her body wrapped around me. Heaven. This is heaven. But I don't want her wrapped around me because she feels sorry for me. I want her wrapped around me because her body's on fire and I'm the only one who can douse it.

"There was no baby."

She loosens her hold to meet my gaze. "Say what now? There was no baby?"

"She lied," I grit out. "She wanted to marry a rockstar and thought getting pregnant was the golden ticket."

"Bitch."

I don't disagree.

"I'm confused why you're telling me this," Leia says when the silence begins to stretch.

"My fucked up past is why I was such an asshat to you in the beginning."

She raises her eyebrows. I should have known she wouldn't let me off easy. Nothing's easy with Leia and I wouldn't have it any other way.

"I wanted you from the moment I saw you. Your blonde hair was flying in the wind behind you and you were giggling and carefree. You were irresistible. But I knew better. Women always betray you."

"Always?"

"That's what I thought. But not anymore."

She squeezes my bicep before stepping back. "I appreciate you trusting me with your past, but I don't have time for dating at the moment. I'm going to go find Isla now. You okay?"

"I'm okay."

Leia waves as she leaves. I'm not deterred she turned me down. I was a complete and total asshat to her when we met. She needs time to realize I'm a man she can trust.

Since we finished recording our album, I have nothing but time.

Chapter 14

Girls' night – an excuse to dig into your friend's past

LEIA

"*his face the color of sodden ashes.*"

I glance over at Isla as I swipe the page to the next chapter of *The Sweetness of the Bottom of the Pie*. I sigh in relief when I notice she's asleep. We spent a good fifteen minutes arguing about whether she's old enough for this book by Alan Bradley.

The recommended age is fourteen but my daughter was determined. Everyone she knows has read it. After reading the first chapter aloud to her, I sincerely doubt any of her friends have read this book.

The doorbell rings and I jump from my spot on Isla's bed to rush and answer it.

"Girls' night!" Indigo shouts when I open the door.

I step onto the porch and shut the door behind me. "Keep your voice down. Isla's asleep."

"Girls' night!" Indigo whisper-shouts.

"Told you this was a bad idea," Virginia says.

"You're only saying it's a bad idea because you don't want to leave your house after eight at night," Indigo claims.

"I was reading a book."

"What book?" I ask. I wouldn't have a clue about the book since I don't have time to read anything other than pre-teen books for Isla, but it's fun to tease Indigo by getting off track.

"*A Court of—*"

Indigo slashes her hand in the air to cut Virginia off. "No!"

"No what?"

"No, you aren't going to distract me from my mission."

I frown. "Mission?"

"Yes, mission. We can do it here or at the bar. Your choice."

I haven't known Indigo long but I'd be a fool not to recognize the determination in her eyes. I might as well get this over with now. Besides, my plan for this evening was to review some spreadsheets. This can't be any worse.

"You can come inside to discuss whatever this mission is, but I'm warning you. If you wake Isla, I'm going to douse your panties in honey and sic a swarm of bees on you."

Indigo grins. "Cruel. I love it."

She pushes past me to traipse inside.

Virginia pats my arm as she passes me. "Don't worry. We won't wake Isla."

"Do you want a drink?" I ask once they're settled on the sofa.

"Would it be a girls' night without drinks?" Indigo asks.

"I have juice or milk. I don't have any beer or wine."

"Not a problem." Indigo pulls a bottle of red wine out of her bag. "I came prepared."

I grab three glasses from the kitchen. I sit on the chair across from the sofa while Indigo pours the wine.

"To friends!" she says as she lifts her glass.

"What's this mission?" I ask once I've taken my first sip of wine.

"Getting straight to business, are we?" Indigo asks.

"I have work to do, Virginia has a book to read, and you have a rockstar to get back to."

"Nope. My rockstar is currently hanging with your rockstar."

"I don't have a rockstar."

But you want to.

I ignore my inner voice. She's unreliable when it comes to men.

"Why not?" Indigo asks.

"Leave her alone. She doesn't have to spill her secrets to you," Virginia says.

Indigo's brow wrinkles. "But she's one of my besties. Besties tell each other everything."

"Why are we besties again?" I mutter.

Indigo wags her finger at me. "Don't act as if you don't love me. I know you love me."

"I barely know you."

She shrugs. "Your love for me will only grow from now on."

Virginia sighs. "I apologize for her. Hanging around small children all day has clearly affected her ability to behave as an adult."

"You can't apologize for me. An apology doesn't mean anything if it's not sincere." Indigo pauses. "And I'm not sorry."

"Of course, you aren't," Virginia grumbles. "You won't be satisfied until every single member of *Cash & the Sinners* is paired with a woman you consider your sister."

"I have a mission," Indigo says.

I hold up my hand. "Count me out of this mission. I am not interested in any of the members of the band."

Liar.

"Not even Fender?" Indigo wiggles her eyebrows.

"Especially not Fender."

"Rumor has it he asked you out."

I don't bother asking her how she knows. I may not have lived in a small town before but I understand rumor mills after having been the object of the high school rumor mill. At least this rumor is true. The rumor I was probed by an alien and got pregnant was not.

"And I said no."

"But why?" She pouts.

"Have you met Fender? He doesn't merely live in Grumpsville. He's been crowned the king of Grumpsville Land."

"He's not as grumpy around you."

I roll my eyes. "Not as grumpy doesn't mean not grumpy."

"Who cares if he's grumpy? He's hot."

"Being sexy doesn't negate his grumpiness."

"Aha!" She motions toward me and ends up spilling her wine on her shirt. "You admit he's sexy."

I shrug. I'm not going to deny the obvious. And, trust me, it is obvious how sexy Fender is. The expression tall, dark, and handsome was invented especially for him. What I wouldn't do to dig my hands into those wide shoulders while he lifts me up and pushes me against the nearest surface.

"Earth to Leia!" Indigo cries.

Any sexy thoughts involving Fender disappear from my mind at how loud she was.

"If you woke up Isla, you're the one who's putting her back to bed and dealing with her in the morning when she's snarly from not getting enough sleep."

Sorry, she mouths.

I set my wine on the table and go to check on my daughter. I creep down the hallway. When I stop in front of her bedroom, Indigo bumps into me.

I glare at her. "What are you doing?"

"Checking on Isla."

I place a finger over my lips before opening the door. Isla is curled up in her bed, cuddling the stuffed horse Fender bought her the day we went for a trail ride. I shut the door and creep back down the hallway.

"You are one lucky woman," I tell Indigo once we're settled back in the living room.

She grins. "I am. Have you seen my boyfriend?"

"Dylan is way sexier than Cash."

They're both wrong. Fender is the sexiest member of the band. The other four can't hold a candle to him. Especially when he brings out the dimples. Sexy hot and dimples is one lethal combination.

Indigo clears her throat. "Leia thinks Fender's the sexiest."

I scowl. "Do not."

"Liar."

"I hate to agree with Indigo on pretty much anything," Virginia begins. "But it is obvious you think Fender is hot. Why don't you want to go out with him? Are you worried about him being a rockstar? I was worried about Dylan not wanting me since I'm a lowly librarian and he's this big hot-shot rocker."

"I don't care if Fender is a rockstar. I don't want to date him. End of story."

"Sure, you don't. What bologna excuses did you give Fender when you told him no?" Indigo asks.

"They're not bologna excuses."

"Let's hear them."

"He thinks I'm a crappy mom."

Indigo narrows her eyes on me. "Anyone with eyes can see you're a great mom. Did he actually say you're a bad mom?"

He did.

And he apologized.

"He also thinks I work too hard."

Indigo motions to the computer and papers on the coffee table. "He might have a point about the overworking thing."

Virginia stands. "I believe we're finished here."

"We are not finished."

"Leia explained her reasons for not wanting to date Fender. Mission accomplished."

Indigo grabs Virginia's arm and pulls her back down. "She's making excuses. I want to know the real reason she said no."

I consider fighting with her, but she's right. The reasons I named are excuses. I can't keep using them after Fender apologized. "I don't want a relationship."

"Why not?"

"I don't have time for a man," I hedge.

Indigo wiggles her eyebrows. "You can use him for sex."

"I'm not the type of person who can use a man for sex."

I've never actually tried it before, but I doubt it's a good idea to use Fender for sex when I can't stop thinking about the man as it is. If he rocks my world, I'll probably become obsessed.

"Why don't you go out on one date with him?" Virginia suggests. "You don't have to have sex with him. Go on a date and let whatever happens happen."

Good idea.

Oh, shush, Ms. Inner Voice of Bad Ideas. It's not happening.

Why not?

Because.

Because you like him and won't admit it to yourself.

Damnit. I hate when she's right. She's the worst gloater.

"And if the date turns into a relationship..." Virginia shrugs.

I scowl. A relationship? Nope. I don't want one of those. Especially since relationships with men always end in heartbreak.

Chapter 15

Child – A small person who can claim to hate you as much as they want but you'll still love her no matter what

LEIA

"Mom!" Isla shouts as if I'm on the other side of Colorado instead of at my desk working three feet away from her.

I swallow my irritation. It's not her fault I'm still working.

"Yes, my beloved daughter."

"Can I go to the movies?"

I shut my laptop to focus on my daughter. In my experience, this sort of question often leads to a discussion. Assuming screaming, whining, and tears is a discussion.

"With whom?"

"Storm and my other friends from the community center."

I'm glad she's made friends at the center. Starting school next month at a new school in a new town will be easier if she already has friends in the same grade as her.

"Where is the movie?"

Winter Falls doesn't have a movie theater. It's too small of a town to have one, although there is a movie night at the library every month. Those movies are not meant for eleven-year-olds though. No matter how much the eleven-year-old in question thinks she's an adult.

"In White Bridge."

White Bridge is a town about thirty minutes away from Winter Falls. It's much bigger and has many of the amenities we lack here.

"How are you planning to get there?" There isn't exactly a bus service around here.

"Storm's mom is driving us."

I've met Storm, but I've yet to meet her mom.

"I'll need to phone her to check she's okay driving you to the movies."

"Mom," Isla whines. "You'll embarrass me."

Too bad for my daughter I don't care how embarrassing she thinks I am. "Your safety trumps me embarrassing you every single day."

"If Storm's mom says it's okay, I can go?"

Not so quick, my little schemer. "What movie are you going to?"

She mumbles her answer.

"Can you repeat yourself at a volume normal humans can hear?"

"*Blood Rave.*"

Blood Rave? My eyes widen. I haven't heard of the movie, but the title does not bode well. I open my laptop to research it.

"What are you doing? Are you ignoring me?"

"I wouldn't dare ignore you, my precious daughter. I'm checking whether the movie is appropriate for your age before I agree."

"It's appropriate."

I'll decide for myself, little Miss manipulator.

I type the title in the search bar and the movie immediately pops up. When I see the movie poster and the content rating, I don't bother reading the blurb.

"It's PG-13."

"I'm almost thirteen."

"Eleven is—

"Eleven and three-quarters," Isla interrupts me to say.

She was eleven and a half yesterday. Still. "Eleven and three-quarters is not thirteen."

I'm grateful she's not thirteen because I wouldn't want her watching this movie at sixteen, let alone thirteen. Judging by the poster, this movie is scary and Isla has nightmares whenever we watch anything remotely scary.

Isla stomps her foot. "But Storm's mom will be there. I'll be with an adult."

"I'm sorry, Isla. The answer is no."

"I hate you! You never let me do anything I want to!" she screeches before marching away.

I sigh before standing to follow her. I won't yell at her for claiming to hate me but I won't allow her to yell at me either.

She flies out of the back door and races toward Fender's house where the band is gathered around the firepit in the backyard. Cash is singing low while Dylan plays his guitar and

Jett taps on an upside-down bucket with his drumsticks. I pause to listen.

She's a fire in the night,
A force that burns so bright,
She calls to me,
In her eyes, I see the key.
With every move she makes,
My heart begins to ache,
She's the melody I crave,
In her arms, I can be brave.

I haven't heard this song before. It must be a new one for their upcoming album. Sounds like another hit to me, but what do I know?

"Fender!" Isla shouts to interrupt them. She barrels into him and he picks her up and places her on his lap.

"What's up, cutie pie?"

"Mom's being mean."

He searches the area until he finds me. He raises an eyebrow and I shake my head.

He returns his attention to my daughter. "She is? What did she do?"

"She won't let me go to the movies with my friends."

"Why not?"

"Because she hates me." Isla bursts into tears.

"Now, now." Fender wipes her tears away and I nearly swoon at the gentle way he handles my child.

Despite having sworn off relationships, I've always wanted a father for Isla. I've spent countless nights awake in bed feeling guilty she doesn't have a father after another asshole kid in her class teased her about not having a dad.

"I don't think your mom hates you."

"She won't let me go to the movies," Isla pouts with her bottom lip stuck out.

"Did she say why she doesn't want you going to the movies?"

Isla crosses her arms over her chest and refuses to answer.

"Was it because you didn't clean your room?"

She shakes her head.

"Was it because you didn't do the dishes?"

She glances away.

"Was it because you didn't do your other chores?"

"I cleaned my room and did all my chores and she still won't let me go to the movies!" Isla screeches.

"What movie do you want to see?" Jett asks.

I narrow my eyes on him. "If you offer to take her to the movies after I told her no, I'm going to break those sticks of yours and shove them somewhere deeply unpleasant."

Gibson chuckles. "How do you know he'll find it unpleasant? He is a daredevil."

I wag my finger at him. "Don't you start. I can cut off your beer supply with one phone call."

He clutches his chest. "You wouldn't!"

"Try me."

"You're mean."

I'm about done with people calling me mean today. I'm not looking forward to Isla becoming a teenager.

"I'm a single mom trying to raise a daughter," I remind him.

"Sorry," Jett says. "I shouldn't have interfered."

I nod to indicate I accept his apology.

"Isla." I hold my hand out to her. "Why don't we go home and stop bothering the neighbors?"

"I'm not bothering Fender," she claims.

Fender smiles at me and those dimples come out. I glare at him. He knows exactly how I feel about those dimples. He shrugs. He obviously isn't feeling the least bit guilty.

"I can't jam around the firepit anyway," he says. "There's a town ordinance about using an amp outside."

I snort. He has no idea what he's done. Isla will never stop bothering him now that he's practically given her permission.

"Come on, Isla. We can make some cookies and watch a movie at home."

"I don't want to watch a movie with you! I want to watch a movie with my friends!"

She's a pre-teen. She doesn't mean those words, I remind myself.

"You're not watching a PG-13 movie when you're eleven."

"Fender would let me." She bats her eyelashes at him. "Wouldn't you?"

He tweaks her nose. "Sorry, cutie pie. If your mom says no, the answer's no."

My heart pounds in my chest. Fender is supporting me? He's not using the situation to his advantage? Was I wrong about him?

"B-b-but..." A tear leaks from Isla's eye and he wipes it away.

"But I will come over and watch a movie with you at your house. Assuming your mom says it's okay."

"Mom!" Isla hollers. "Fender's coming over to watch a movie."

I cross my arms over my chest. "Those words did not resemble a question."

She scrunches up her eyes and does her best to glare at me. I don't give in. I learned my lesson about giving in more than six years ago. Spoiler alert – it's never just one candy with a five-year-old.

"Can Fender come over and watch a movie with us?"

I raise my eyebrows and she huffs.

"Can Fender come over and watch a movie with us, please?"

I nod. "Yes, Fender can come over."

"Yeah!" She jumps off his lap and holds out her hand to him. He doesn't hesitate to take it.

"What movie are we watching?" he asks as they walk across the yard hand in hand.

I worry my lip as I observe them. Fender supported me, he didn't pressure me to do what Isla wanted, and he comforted my daughter.

Maybe I can give him a chance.

After all, how much harm can one date do?

Chapter 16

Cookies – an excuse to maneuver yourself to where you want to be

FENDER

"Do you know how to make cookies?" Isla asks as we enter her house.

"I do."

Leia rushes in behind us. "Sorry. I wasn't expecting visitors," she says as she hurries to gather the papers scattered on the kitchen table.

I shackle her wrist to stop her. "Do you need to work? I can come back later."

She snorts and waves to Isla who's already pulling out ingredients to make cookies. "There's no way my daughter is letting you leave. She'd handcuff herself to you if she could."

The only person I want handcuffed to me is Leia. Although, I prefer to do the handcuffing. I have to hold back a groan at the vision of Leia spread-eagle on the bed with her hands tied to the headboard. She'd be at my mercy. My pants tighten as my cock enjoys the vision.

"Fender!" Isla hollers.

I clear my throat and force my mind away from sexy images of my little firecracker.

"You're certain I'm not interrupting your work?" I ask Leia.

"It's fine. Go help my daughter bake cookies before her head explodes."

I chuckle and do as she says.

Isla already has the baking sheet on the counter along with a roll of pre-made chocolate chip cookie dough.

I tap the dough. "This is cheating."

"It is?"

"Do you have chocolate chips?" I ask.

By the time Leia returns to the kitchen – her hair combed and wearing a different outfit – we're nearly finished.

"You're making cookies from scratch?" she asks as I demonstrate to Isla how to drop a rounded tablespoon of batter onto the cookie sheet.

"Look Mom!" Isla dips a tablespoon into the dough. When she lifts it, she brings out nearly half of the dough mixture.

"That's a bit too much, cutie pie." I snatch the spoon from her and show her again how much dough to use.

"I got it!" Isla tries to plop the dough onto the cookie sheet except the dough doesn't leave the spoon. She shakes the spoon and this time the dough does leave the spoon. It doesn't land on the cookie sheet, though. It flies through the air and lands on Leia's chin.

Isla's eyes widen. "Uh-oh."

Leia wipes the dough away from her face and it falls to the counter. "Now you know why we use the pre-made dough."

"I'm sorry," I say. "I didn't think."

"Or you thought I needed a facial."

"You don't need a facial. You're perfect."

She scowls. "I don't deserve to treat myself to a facial?"

"I-I…" I hold my hands up and back away. Shit. I screwed up.

She glares at me for a few seconds before bursting into laughter. "You." She points at me. "You're so easy."

For her, I'm easy. Not for anyone else.

I grab a towel and wet it. Leia nabs it from me before I can clean her face. I scowl. I want to take care of her. She doesn't have to do everything by herself.

"All done," Isla declares.

The cookie sheet has eight blobs instead of twelve spoonfuls of dough, but I'm not complaining. I place it in the oven and set the timer.

"What movie should we watch?" I ask.

"*Spy Kids: Armageddon!*"

"I haven't seen it."

Isla's eyes widen. "You haven't seen it?"

"No."

"Have you seen any of the Spy Kids movies?"

I don't even know what the Spy Kids movies are. "No."

"Yippee! We can start from the beginning," she says, and Leia moans.

"What's wrong?" I whisper to Leia when Isla is in the living room.

"I've seen those movies a million times. The joys of being a parent."

I wouldn't mind watching a movie a million times. It's a small price to pay in my opinion. My face must give me away because she grabs my wrists.

"I'm sorry. I'm being insensitive."

"It's fine."

"No, it's not." She clears her throat. "And I should also make it clear I accept your apology."

"You do?"

She narrows her eyes on me. "No using the dimples."

"Didn't realize I was."

"You're trouble."

"But I'm the good kind."

"There's a good kind?"

I bend close to whisper into her ear. "I'll show you."

She shivers. I long to pull her into my arms. If whispering in her ear causes her to shiver, I want to experience how she responds to my tongue or my fingers on her body.

The doorbell rings before I can put those plans into action.

"I'll get it," Isla shouts, and Leia hurries after her.

Run away, Leia. Run away. Running only makes me want to chase you more.

I follow. Of course, I follow. I want to follow Leia wherever she goes.

"Hi Storm," Isla greets a girl on the doorstep.

"You must be Leia," the woman next to Storm says. "I'm Honor." She turns to greet me and her eyes widen. "And who's this?" she asks as she rakes her gaze up and down me.

I grunt.

Leia waves a hand toward me. "This is Grumpy Pants Mac-Grumpy."

Honor licks her bottom lip. "I can handle a bit of grumpy."

Leia steps in front of me. The move is possessive. Is she jealous? I cough to hide my smirk. Me smirking at her show of jealousy would piss her off. Although, I do enjoy a pissed off Leia.

"I'm sorry but Isla's not allowed to attend the movie."

Honor sighs. "I know. Someone," she glares at her daughter, "didn't tell me which movie they wanted to see."

"It's not a big deal," Isla and Storm say together.

"What are you doing here if you're not picking up Isla for the movie?" Leia asks.

"I thought Isla might want to come over and have dinner with us," Honor says.

"Yeah!" Isla jumps up and down before rushing out of the house holding hands with Storm.

"Isla!" Leia calls after her. "Did you forget something?"

Isla glances down at her feet. "Nope."

Leia crosses her arms over her chest. "Try again."

Isla sighs. "Please, Mom, can I go to Storm's house for dinner?"

"Do you really want two tweens in your house at once?" Leia asks Honor.

Honor snorts in response. "I have two teenage boys at home. I can handle two tween girls."

"If she's any trouble, give me a ring and I'll come pick her up."

"I will. Nice meeting you." Honor waves as she leaves with the girls.

Leia shuts the door after her. "You know what this means?"

I have a whole bunch of ideas of what this could mean. "What?"

Leia's eyes sparkle. "We get to eat all the cookies."

I step closer. I'm down with eating all of her cookies.

The kitchen timer buzzes and she hurries to the kitchen. Oh, those cookies.

She removes the baking sheet from the oven and sets it on the stove. She frowns at the lump-sized cookies. "I don't think my daughter is going to be a baker."

I snag a cookie and bite into it. It's a bit hot but the flavor is fine. "Tastes good to me."

She hands me a glass of milk. "Sorry, I don't have any asbestos for your throat."

I shrug as I drink my milk. "Hot food doesn't bother me."

"Alrighty then, Superman. Are you also wearing tight leggings under your jeans?"

"I'm not Superman, but I am pretty strong."

Her gaze dips to my chest and her eyes heat.

"Will you go out on a date with me?"

"What?" I must be hearing things. The last I remember Leia didn't want to date me, but now she's asking me out. When did things change?

"Do I have to spell things out for you? Will you?" She pokes me in the chest. "Go out with me?"

I growl. "I understood."

"Good. Now answer the question."

"No."

She rears back. "No? What the hell? You literally asked me out two days ago and now you don't want to date me? What's wrong with you? Did you meet some other woman in the meantime? Don't want to lower yourself to a single mom? Or is it—"

I do the one thing guaranteed to shut her up. I palm her neck and draw her near before slamming my lips on hers. She gasps and I take advantage by shoving my tongue into her mouth. The second her tart lemon taste hits me, I'm lost.

I want to taste every inch of her mouth before moving on to other parts of her body. I thread my hands through her hair to bring her closer. Until her chest touches mine and I can feel her gasping for air.

Her hands lift to grasp my shoulders. Her nails dig into my skin through my t-shirt as her tongue duels with mine.

I groan and use my hold on her to tilt her head so I can dive in deeper. I press my hard cock against her belly and her fingers tighten on my shoulders. I can't wait to get her in bed. Get her naked and experience how every inch of her tastes.

Her phone rings and she wrenches her lips from mine. Her mouth is swollen from my kisses, her hair is a mess from my hands, and her eyes are dark with passion. She couldn't be sexier if she tried.

"I need to…" She doesn't finish the sentence before hurrying away.

I let her go. For now. She'll be mine soon enough.

I adjust my cock in my pants before leaving out the back door.

I'll be back, Leia. I hope she's ready for all I plan to give her.

Chapter 17

Asshat – Not to be confused with a dumbass

FENDER

"Are you awake, Fender?" Stan, our producer, asks through the microphone.

"I'm awake," I grumble.

But this studio is not where I want to be. I want to be at Leia's house. I never got a chance to explain why I said no when she asked me out. I should have stayed and waited for her to finish her call.

"I'm with him," Jett hollers.

"I'm with Grumpapottamus, too," Gibson agrees. "I don't understand what we're doing here."

I slam my bass down before marching toward Gibson. "Not grumpapottamus."

Dylan steps in front of Gibson. "No fighting."

I glare at Gibson who ducks behind Dylan. "Someone save me from the grump monster."

"Enough!" Cash growls. "I told you the studio asked us to record two more songs for a special edition album."

"If everyone would behave, we'd have these songs done in no time," Dylan adds.

Gibson peeks his head out from behind Dylan's back. "It's not my fault Fender can't take a joke."

Dylan cocks an eyebrow. "And at no time did you think 'Hey, Fender, is extra grumpy today? Maybe I shouldn't call him a ridiculous name?'"

"He is extra grumpy today," Jett says as he taps out a beat on his drums. "Extra grumpy, extra grumpy. Is grumpapottamus feeling extra horny today?"

"Leia turned you down, did she?" Gibson asks.

I cross my arms over my chest and growl at him. He squeaks before hiding behind Dylan's back again.

The door to the studio slams open and our producer charges inside. "Are we doing a fucking therapy session or are we recording music?"

Cash blocks him. "No. This is band business. Out."

"I can hear everything you say from in there anyway." Stan waves toward the control room.

Cash nods to Rob, our studio engineer, and he cuts the sound between the two rooms. "I told you when you demanded we record two more songs there would be issues."

"This isn't about the music."

"I never said the issues would be about the music."

"Fucking musicians," Stan mutters before stomping out of the studio.

"Now," Cash begins. "Is everyone going to behave so we can finish recording this song sometime this century?"

"I always behave," Jett claims.

"When? When do you behave?" Cash asks.

Jett shrugs. "I always follow the instructions for hooking up my parachute."

"Can we finish this recording and get out of here?" I growl.

"Uh-oh. Big guy's getting impatient. Better get back to it before his grumpiness explodes," Gibson says.

My nostrils flare as I stare at him while debating whether I should pick him up and throw him against the wall or get this recording over so I can go to Leia's house and figure out where her head's at.

Leia wins. She'll always win with me. I grab my bass.

Cash rubs his hands together. "Let's do this!"

Easy for him to be enthusiastic. He's going home to the woman he loves. I want what he has. Maybe someday – with Leia – I will.

But I screwed up by leaving yesterday. Is she pissed at me? I need to get to her. My body vibrates with the desire to go to her but I lock it down to finish the recording.

"It's a wrap." The words are barely out of the studio engineer's mouth before I'm moving.

"Where are we going?" Gibson asks as he and Jett follow me.

I increase my pace until they have to run to keep up or fall behind. Naturally, they don't fall behind. I should be so lucky. They jog next to me while throwing questions at me.

"Do you need tips on how to seduce Leia?"

"Or tips for when you're in the bedroom?"

I ignore them and continue until I reach the meadow behind our house.

"What are we doing here?"

"Does he have a shovel?"

"A shovel? What does he need a shovel for?"

"To bury us."

If I was going to kill and bury them, I would have done it the first time I had to escort a drunk and naked woman out of their hotel room.

I search the meadow until I find the flowers I want and gather a bunch.

"Phew. He's not going to kill us. He's picking daisies," Gibson says.

"Not daisies," I grumble as I begin walking to Leia's house.

"Isn't he sweet? He got flowers for his lady," Jett says.

I stop and glare at them. "Stop following me."

"And miss the part where Leia removes your balls with a spoon?" Gibson chuckles. "No way."

"Why would she remove my balls with a spoon?"

Jett motions to the flowers. "You obviously screwed up."

"Fine. What will it take for you to leave me alone?"

Gibson doesn't hesitate. "You to stop hiding my beer."

I scowl. He needs to slow down his drinking. He's careening out of control. But I know better than to tell him. Which is why I started hiding his beer. It doesn't work. He just buys more.

"Fine."

I march away but Jett continues to tag after me.

"What about me, big guy? What do I get?"

"How about I leave you in the field covered in blood the next time you break your leg and the ambulance can't reach you?"

He pales before motioning for me to go ahead without him.

I increase my speed as I make my way to Leia's house anyway since Jett and Gibson are not to be trusted. When I reach the house, I glance around to make certain they haven't followed me. They wave from the front porch of our house. I give them my back and ring the doorbell.

"What is it?" Leia asks when she answers the door.

"These are for you." I hand her the flowers.

"Daisies? You think daisies will cool my anger?"

"They're not daisies. They're Black-eyed Susans, a wild-flower native to Colorado."

Her brow wrinkles. "Are you a botanist on the side?"

"Eden from *Eden's Garden* helped me."

I went to the flower shop next to *Bertie's Recording Studio* to buy Leia flowers but the flower shop doesn't sell flowers. Instead, I got a lecture on the flower industry and how it's ruining the earth. She even had a hand-out to explain things further. A hand-out I was tasked with reading and returning to her at my next opportunity because paper is bad, too.

Winter Falls and all its rules is confusing at times. But there's no place I'd rather be. Not as long as Leia and Isla are here.

"I'll put these in water," Leia says before whirling around.

She leaves the door open so I follow her to the kitchen.

"I'm still mad. I asked you out, you said no, gave me the best kiss of my life, and then you disappeared."

I smirk. "The best kiss of your life?"

She scowls. "Forget what I said."

I stalk to her and she retreats until her back hits the counter. "It was the best kiss of my life, too."

She snorts. "Yeah, right. You're a rockstar. You've probably kissed more women than the combined male population of San Diego."

"No. After Vicki, I stopped fooling around with fans."

Her brow wrinkles. "You did?"

I nod.

"But what about your needs?"

"My hand worked fine." I step closer. Until my chest hits hers. "But not anymore."

"Your hand doesn't work anymore? But you play the bass. You need your hand. Have you seen a specialist?"

I interrupt her before she can start phoning doctors. "I can use my hand but it no longer satisfies my needs."

"Oh." Her mouth forms a perfect circle and I groan as I imagine her mouth wrapped around my cock. Her lips stretched. Those blue eyes hot with passion. My hands fisted in those blonde curls.

"Do you want to go out with me?"

Her eyes flare with anger. "You said no when I asked you out."

"Because I want to be the one to take care of you. To ask you out. To take you out on dates."

She frowns. "That's a good answer."

I grin. "I know."

"No getting cocky, dimple boy."

I widen my smile so both of my dimples pop out.

"You're using your dimples as a weapon again."

"It's only fair since you exist and I'm tempted."

Her breath catches. "W–w–what?"

I lean close to whisper in her ear. "You heard me. You're a walking temptation to me. Even when I was being a dumbass, you tempted me."

"I thought we agreed on the term asshat."

"Asshat then." I take a chance and nip her earlobe. She shivers in response. This woman wants me but she doesn't want to want me. "What do you say, Leia? One date. If it's a disaster, I'll leave you alone. Never bother you again."

It won't be a disaster. And I won't leave her alone. I'll figure out a way to endear myself to her.

"Fine," she grits out.

I kiss the spot below her ear before retreating.

"I'll see you tonight."

"Tonight? But I don't have a babysitter for Isla."

"Let me handle everything."

"This ought to be interesting," she mutters.

"See you tonight," I call as I open the back door. I'm not staying and giving her a chance to change her mind. I can already see her beginning to doubt herself. Not happening.

Chapter 18

Rockstars – Can be babysitters as long as candy's involved

LEIA

I throw the skirt on top of the growing pile of clothes on the bed. What do you wear to a date with a rockstar? When you don't know where you're going? Or what you're doing?

A dress? A skirt? Jeans and a blouse?

Why is this so hard? I'm twenty-nine years old. I am not a teenager going to a dance with the captain of the football team.

I pick out a summer skirt with a t-shirt. If it's not good enough, it's Fender's fault for refusing to answer my question on what we're doing. Spoiler alert: Telling a woman it's a surprise is not a good idea when she doesn't know what to wear.

The doorbell rings and I rush from my room to answer it but I don't manage to get there before Isla.

"Fender!" She greets as I reach the entryway.

He ruffles her hair. "Hey, cutie pie."

"Are you here to watch a movie with us?"

"Nope. I have something better."

"Something better?"

"Yep. Something better." Fender's gaze meets mine and his eyes heat. "Assuming your mom approves."

Damn it. He knows exactly how to make me weak in the knees. Kindness to my kid will do it every time.

Isla bounces on her toes. "Can I, Mom? Can I?"

"Can you what?" I ask. "We don't know what Fender has planned for you yet."

He holds out his hand. "I'll show you."

Isla takes his hand and he tugs her out of the house. He waits until I follow before leading her across our yard to his house. My brow furrows. What is he up to?

We stop at the door to his house. "Keep an open mind." He waits until I nod before opening the door.

Isla rushes inside and squeals. I start to follow her but Fender shackles my wrist to stop me. He kisses my nose. "An open mind, yeah?"

He draws me into the room and I gasp. There are fairy lights strung up along the walls, a pink tent set up in front of the television, and snacks set out on trays on the floor.

"Mom," Isla calls from inside the tent.

I get on my knees and crawl inside. There are pillows and blankets spread out on the floor. Isla's already lying under a blanket.

"Isn't this the best?"

"You like it?" Jett asks as he lays down beside Isla.

Gibson rolls his eyes. "Of course, she likes it. It's awesome."

Isla giggles at Gibson.

"She laughed. She likes it."

Fender sticks his head in the tent. "Gibson and Jett are going to keep an eye on Isla while we go on our date. Assuming you're okay with it."

"Why wouldn't she be okay with it?" Gibson asks. "We're awesome."

"And we have the best treats."

"Maybe too much food." I motion to the pizza, chicken wings, brownies, and gummy bears stacked on trays in front of the tent.

Gibson smacks Jett. "Told you it was too much."

Jett ducks his head but not before I notice the blush on his cheeks. "I wanted her to have her favorites but Fender said we couldn't ask her any questions."

I squeeze his shoulder. "It's okay. This is a special occasion. But don't let her eat too much. She'll get sick."

"Got it."

Fender offers me his hand. "Ready?"

I glare at Jett and Gibson one last time. "If anything happens to Isla in your care, I will post about your competition to sleep with the most fans on social media."

"Okay," Jett immediately agrees while Gibson gapes at me.

Good enough. I clasp Fender's hand and he helps me to stand.

He draws me into his arms. "You're certain you're okay with this arrangement?"

"I couldn't drag Isla away now if I wanted to."

He tucks a strand of hair behind my ear. "Then, it's time for our date. You ready?"

I gulp. "Yep."

I say my good-byes to my daughter and Fender's bandmates before he leads me outside. I gasp when I notice the vehicle waiting for us at the curb.

"Holy cow, Fender."

He shrugs. "I'm a big guy. I need a big car."

"But a Hummer? Is this thing even allowed in Winter Falls?"

"It's electric," he says as he opens the door for me.

I stare at the seat. It's nearly as high as my chest. Am I supposed to climb into this? Fender solves the problem when he lifts me up and places me on the seat.

"You didn't have to lift me." I would have figured out how to climb in. Eventually.

He leans over me to click on my seatbelt. "I enjoy carrying you, firecracker."

"Firecracker?"

He grins and one of his dimples pops out. It's amazing really. One dimple and his face goes from grumpy to sexy. Although, his grumpy face is pretty sexy, too.

"Are you going to deny you're a firecracker?"

He has a point. "Nope."

Once we're on the road out of Winter Falls, I ask, "Where are we going?"

"It's a surprise."

I hate surprises. I prefer to be prepared for every possible contingency. How can I be prepared if I don't know what's going to happen?

Fender reaches across the center console and squeezes my thigh. "Don't worry. You'll enjoy it."

I open my mouth to ask him how he knows when he continues, "I hope."

The uncertainty in his voice has me shutting my mouth. He's nervous. It's endearing. And annoying since I can no longer bug him to tell me what the surprise is.

"How was your day?" he asks.

"How was my day?" I repeat.

"Yeah. How was your day? Did your boss drive you batty? Did you finish all your work before I picked you up?"

No one's ever asked me how my day was before. I've been on my own since my grandparents died when Isla was three. There's never been anyone waiting for me when I came home from work – except Isla.

I would do anything for my daughter, but I have missed adult conversation at home. Being able to bitch about my boss without worrying the language I'm using will scare my daughter for life would be nice.

"Work was okay today," I finally manage to say. "Brody actually said thank you."

Fender scowls. "Does he not thank you for the work you do more often?"

"Ha! Let me tell you about the time I refused to talk to him for a week because he didn't say thank you. He had no clue what was happening."

By the time I finish my story, Fender is pulling into a parking lot.

"Where are we?" I ask as I gaze around. The building in front of us reminds me of a castle from a Disney movie. The 'castle' is surrounded by nature, and the parking lot is full of fancy cars. Wherever we are, I don't think I belong here.

"Um…"

Fender's cheeks heat as he stumbles over his words.

"You said something about deserving time to pamper yourself the other day so I asked Virginia how I could pamper you."

"Virginia?"

"Indigo's a blabber mouth. She would have told everyone in Winter Falls what we're doing."

"Pamper me?"

"I know being a single mom isn't easy. I was raised by one."

"Hold on. You were? Why didn't you say anything?"

He shrugs. "I assumed you knew."

"Because you're a famous rockstar and I should follow your every move in the tabloids and on social media?" I roll my eyes. Who has the time?

He chuckles. "Sorry. Sometimes I forget how unimpressed you are with my status."

"Anyway, you were raised by a single mom?"

"It's a story for another day."

I open my mouth to berate him but stop when I remember pushing someone to tell their secrets never works. I was a stubborn teenager once too.

"You want to pamper me?"

"You deserve it. You work hard, you're raising Isla on your own and doing a damn good job, too."

Oh, how he's changed his tune since we met. "How are you planning to pamper me?"

"Well." He clears his throat. "I thought about sending you for a day at a spa, but I wanted to do something together."

"And?"

"We're doing a couples massage."

"A couples massage?"

"If you don't want to do it, we don't have to. We can skip it and go straight to dinner. I'll cancel the appointment."

He digs in his pocket for his phone but I shackle his wrist.

"You are not denying me my first professional massage."

"You like the idea?"

"I love the idea." I reach for the door handle. "Let's go."

"Wait for me to open your door."

"What? You don't think I can jump down?"

"I know you can, but I don't want you to have to."

Holy cow. Have sexier words ever been uttered? He knows I'm a strong woman but he wants to help me anyway.

Oh boy. I better secure the cage around my heart because I could fall in love with this man. Which would be a stupid thing to do. Because no matter how much I try to ignore it, he's still a rockstar and I'm still a single mom. These two things do not go together.

Chapter 19

Take a chance – do something super scary even when your heart is yelling run

LEIA

I hope you slept well.

Have a good day.

Happiness spreads through me as I read the messages from Fender. Ever since our first date, he sends me these messages in the morning. And every night he messages me to ask me how my day was.

These simple messages are breaking down my resistance to the man.

Why are you still resisting him?

Gah. Sometimes I hate my inner voice. How dare she make me question myself and my decisions? Doesn't she remember what happened the last time I was in a relationship? With Isla's dad?

Fender is not Charles.

Charles – always Charles, never Charlie – was a waste of space. I can't believe I fell for his smooth lines and sweet talk.

Fender is definitely not a sweet talker and he probably wouldn't know a smooth line if it hit him in the face.

Fender's also a gentleman. A word I doubt Charles has ever heard of. Fender brought me home after our date, kissed me on the cheek, and left. He didn't try to push me into having sex with him. Although very little pushing would have been necessary. The man makes my panties damp with a grunt.

My phone beeps with another message. *I'll be there in a few minutes.*

I check my clock. Shit. I spent the past half hour daydreaming instead of finishing up my work. I rush through my 'must be done today' tasks. I've barely finished the final task when the doorbell rings.

"Hey!" I'm out of breath when I open the door to Fender.

He bends over to kiss my cheek. "Are you ready?"

"Yep."

He nods toward my feet and I realize I'm wearing the bunny slippers Isla gave me for Christmas last year.

I shrug. "You didn't tell me where we're going. Who knows? Maybe bunny slippers are appropriate."

He chuckles. "I guess we can go then." He motions to the Hummer.

"Did you buy the Hummer?" I ask as I kick off my bunny loafers and slip into a pair of sandals. "I thought it was a rental."

"I'm leasing it."

"Leasing? Can you lease for short-term?"

"It's a six-month lease."

"But won't you be gone as soon as the record is finished?"

"I don't have anywhere else I need to be."

"What about your mom?"

He shrugs. "She won't miss me."

I frown. He told me all about his useless ex-girlfriend, Vicki, but he won't tell me about his mom. Except she was a single mom and apparently won't miss him. I have questions! So many questions.

"Where's Isla?" he asks in an obvious attempt to pre-empt my questions about his mom.

"She's having a sleepover at the community center."

His eyes flare. "A sleepover? She won't be home until morning?"

"Don't get any ideas, big guy," I say despite my mind filling up with tons of ideas. Sexy ideas of him naked in my bed with me. Ideas of me touching every single inch of his skin. And there's a lot of skin to touch.

He growls and grasps my hips to draw me near. "What are you thinking, firecracker?"

My face warms. "Um…"

His fingers squeeze my hip. "Never mind. Your face doesn't lie."

He trails his nose along my neck until he reaches my ear. "I will fulfill all those fantasies you're imagining and then some."

"And then some?" I gasp.

He nips my earlobe. "And then some."

"What if I have a very active imagination?"

"Then, we're going to have a very long, satisfying night."

Warmth spreads from my stomach down to my core where wetness gathers in my panties. Oh my. No man has caused me to get wet merely from speaking. What will Fender do when he gets me into his bed? And how long do I have to wait?

My phone buzzes in my back pocket and I jump in surprise. I giggle at myself before digging my phone out. I frown when I read the screen.

"It's the community center."

I walk away to answer the phone, but Fender follows me and shuts the door behind him.

"Hello," I answer.

"I'm sorry, Leia, but I'm afraid Isla's sick. Can you pick her up?" Cedar, the director of the community center, asks.

"Of course. I'm on my way."

I hang up and rush to the front door. Fender stops me.

"What's happening? Where are you going?"

I yank my arm away from him. "Isla. She's sick."

He grasps my hand and laces my fingers through his. "Come on. We'll get there faster in the Hummer."

I give in since he's right. We're at the community center in a little over a minute. I jump out of the Hummer before Fender can help me. I sprint to the front door with him on my heels.

"Where is she?" I ask when I enter the building.

The place is crowded with kids in their pajamas. I scan the room but I don't see her anywhere. Panic begins to crawl up my throat.

"There she is." Fender points to my daughter helping Storm out of the bathroom.

I rush to her. "Get your things."

"I'll get them," Fender offers.

Isla glances back and forth between me and Fender. "Hold on. Why are you getting my things? What's wrong? Did someone die?"

"You're sick. I'm taking you home."

"I'm not sick. Storm is." She scowls at her friend. "I told you not to eat the entire roll of cookie dough."

"Do you need us to take Storm home?" Fender asks while I'm still trying to process my daughter's words. She's not sick? She's okay?

"My mom's here." Storm waves to Honor who is hurrying toward us.

"Sorry about this," Honor says as she helps Storm away.

I place a palm over Isla's forehead. "You're certain you're feeling okay?"

She swats my hand away. "I'm fine."

"Do you want to come home or stay here?" I ask.

"I have other friends here." She motions to a group of girls huddled on top of their sleeping bags in a far corner.

"You sure?" Fender asks before I have a chance to. "We can watch a movie together."

Is he serious? He's willing to give up a date with me to spend time with my daughter? I thought he wanted some alone time with me.

"Thanks, Fender. But I'm busy tonight."

My heart swells with pride. My daughter isn't rushing to change her plans to spend time with a man. Good for her. She's going to be a wonderful woman some day. A strong woman who doesn't allow a man to hurt her the way I did.

"We'll make plans for another night next week."

"Okay. I gotta go." Isla rushes off without a backward glance.

Fender grasps my hand, leads me out of the center, and helps me into the passenger seat of the Hummer.

"You okay?" he asks as he secures my seatbelt around me.

"As long as Isla's fine, I'm fine."

He kisses my nose before shutting my door and rounding the vehicle to get into the driver's seat.

"Do you want to skip our date?" he asks as we drive back to my house. "We can get some takeout and watch a movie."

"You wouldn't be mad?"

His brow furrows. "Why would I be mad?"

"First, I drag you to the community center at breakneck speed and then I cancel our date."

He parks the car in front of my house and turns to look at me. "It's no big deal."

"No big deal? No big deal?" I screech.

He shrugs. "All I did was drive you to the community center."

"You don't get it. No one has helped me with Isla since my grandparents died. Since Isla was three, I've been on my own."

"You're not on your own now."

"For now. Once you leave Winter Falls, I'll be on my own again."

He grasps my chin. "Open your eyes, firecracker. The whole town is here to support you. Virginia and Indigo will babysit your daughter whenever you ask them, and the gossip gals will help out in any way they can."

My belly warms at his words. Is it true? Is the town here to support me?

I shake my head. "I can't chance it."

"Chance what?"

"Them changing their minds."

"Changing their minds? Changing their minds about what?"

"About me. How do I know they won't decide I'm not worth it?"

He growls. "Not worth it? Firecracker, you're worth everything."

I glance away. "I thought I was once. I thought my parents would support me being pregnant. But no, they kicked me out. I thought Charles would help me raise our child. But, no, he left when Isla was barely five months old."

"What about your grandparents? Didn't they help out?"

"Isla and I lived with them until they passed away."

"They didn't leave you."

"Everyone else did," I mutter.

"Remember how I said all women betray you. And you pointed out I couldn't say *all* women betray you when I really meant Vicki."

I narrow my eyes on him. "Yes."

"If I can't use Vicki's behavior as an excuse to not connect with people, you're not allowed to use your parents and Charles the fuckhead as an excuse."

I throw daggers out of my eyes at him. "I hate it when you use logic."

"Get used to it, firecracker. I'm not going anywhere."

Really? He's not going anywhere? He's staying in Winter Falls? Dare I hope? Nope. I refuse to hope. I snort instead.

"You – a rockstar – are going to stay in Winter Falls forever?"

"Cash and Dylan aren't going anywhere. I'm afraid Jett and Gibson will never leave either." He feigns a shiver. "I'm stuck with Tweedle Dee and Tweedle Dum forever."

He's staying? Hope – an emotion I refuse to allow myself to feel – pushes at my skin as I study his face. Is he being truthful? I'm not the best judge of character. I fell for Charles' bullshit after all. But I was a kid then. Barely old enough to drive. Maybe I should give myself a break. Maybe I should take a chance on another man.

This particular grumpy man to be precise. He was with me one-hundred percent when I thought Isla was sick. He also arranged a babysitter for our first date. And he refused to push it beyond a kiss at the end of the night.

Is Fender Hays the man I've been searching for when I didn't even realize I was searching?

I steel my spine and take a chance. "Do you want to come inside?"

Chapter 20

Come inside – Fender's new favorite two words

FENDER

Do I want to come inside? Hell, yeah, I do.

My cock twitches in response. Leia didn't say come inside her body, I remind it.

I cradle her face with my hands. "Are you sure?"

She laughs. "No."

"Then, no, I don't want to come inside."

Her eyes widen and she slaps my hands away from her face. "What the hell, grumpy man? I invite you inside and you say no!"

She's spitting mad. Daggers shoot from her eyes at me. And her nostrils flare. It's cute. My little firecracker is adorable when she's angry.

I pinch her chin and she snaps her teeth at me. "I'm not coming inside with you until you're sure you want me there. I don't want you to regret anything we do together."

I want her one hundred percent on board with whatever we do.

The anger leaks from her eyes. "I promise I won't regret it."

I pause to study her face. Is she being honest with herself?

"What do you want me to do? Beg?"

I smirk. "Oh, you'll beg, firecracker. And you'll love it, too."

Her eyes narrow. "I doubt it. Are you coming or not?"

Not yet. But I will be coming, firecracker. I will be. And so will you. As many times as you can handle.

"Stay there," I order before jumping out and hurrying around to her side to open her door.

I palm her neck and draw her close. She bites her bottom lip as she stares at my mouth. It's an invitation I can't resist.

I groan as I lean down to meet her lips. I begin slowly – sipping from her lips. I wait until her hands clutch my shoulders before demanding she open for me. She opens with a sigh and I push my tongue into her mouth.

I moan as her taste assaults me. Her tongue darts out to duel with mine but I growl and take over. I fist my hand in her hair and tilt her head to my liking before diving deeper. I can't get enough of her. I will never get enough of her. She moans and digs her fingernails into my shoulders.

I can't wait until we're naked and she's digging into my skin. I want to feel her—

"Yoo! Fender!"

I pull away from Leia to glare at Gibson. He waves from our front porch next door.

"I'm going to kill him," I grumble.

"I'll buy the shovel," Leia adds. Her lips are swollen and her hair is disheveled. It's a good look on her. But I bet naked is a better one.

I throw her over my shoulder and she squeals. "Fender!"

I slap her ass as I shut the car door. "No squirming or I'll drop you."

"Big talker. You would never drop me."

Good. I'm glad she realizes she can trust me to carry her. After tonight she'll also know she can trust me to take care of her in the bedroom.

Leia reaches down to open the door and Gibson hollers, "You're welcome!"

I scowl over at him and he points across the street to where Sage has her binoculars up to her eyes and pointed in our direction. She waves at me before giving me a thumbs-up.

I slam the door shut on both of them. In this house, it's just Leia and me. No one else gets to intrude for the night. Not a gossip gal. Not my bandmates. Not the people of Winter Falls. No one.

"Bedroom?"

Leia motions toward the hallway. I carry her down it and into her room where I lay her on her bed.

"Is this the part where you ravish me?"

I cover her with my body. "Do you want me to ravish you?"

She rolls her eyes. "Duh. Why do you think I invited you inside?"

I drag my teeth along her neck until I reach the juncture with her shoulder and bite down. She moans and arches her back. At the feel of her chest against mine, I realize she's wearing too many clothes.

I get to my knees and reach for the hem of her t-shirt. She slaps my hands away.

"Shouldn't we close the curtains first?"

"The blinds will keep any peeping toms away."

She squirms. "No. I know. I meant…" She bites her lip and looks away.

I clasp her chin. "What did you mean, firecracker?"

"It's still light outside."

"Yep."

She waves a hand down her front. "It's light out."

"Is this code? I don't get it."

"Ugh!" She covers her face with her hands. "It's light out. You can see everything."

"That's the idea, firecracker. I want to see every single inch of your skin. Taste every single inch. Touch every single inch."

Her hands drop from her face. "You do?"

"Every. Single. Inch." I draw my palm up her t-shirt to the underside of her breast.

"What if you don't like what you see?"

My brow furrows. Is she kidding? I'm going to fucking love what I see. I study her face and realize she's serious. This isn't some play to get me to compliment her. She's genuinely nervous.

I lay down next to her on the bed and grasp her hand. "What's wrong?"

"I haven't …erm…you know in a long time."

"Define a long time."

Her hand spasms in mine. "Nine years."

"It's been five years for me."

"What? No way. You're a freaking rockstar. Women throw themselves at you."

"But I don't catch them."

"Are you serious? How is this possible?"

"Easy." I shrug. "I grunt at women when they get too close."

"Grunting didn't keep me away."

"I didn't grunt at you."

"Yes, you did, Grumpy Pants MacGrumpy."

I chuckle. "MacGrumpy? Am I Irish now?"

"Nope. Scottish. Highlanders are sexy."

I smile. Leia's crazy. The good kind. The fun kind. The sexy kind. I've never smiled in bed with a woman before. I like it. I like her.

"Do you want to watch a movie?"

"A movie?"

"Yeah, it's a type of entertainment available on your television."

"Grumpy smartass," she grumbles. "Why would I want to watch television when I have you in my bed?"

"If you're not comfortable taking things to the next level, I can wait."

She climbs on top of me and cradles my face in her hands. "You can wait?"

My cock doesn't understand the concept of waiting. He hardens and lengthens at the feel of the object of our desire on top of us.

Leia straddles me. "It doesn't feel as if you can wait."

"Wanting you doesn't mean I can't wait."

"For someone who doesn't talk much, you sure know the right thing to say at the right time."

I grunt since I have no idea how to respond to her compliment. Guess I don't know the right thing to say at the right time after all.

She giggles. "Grumpy dude is in the house."

I grasp her hips to stop her movements. "I can wait but I will be grumpy if you keep wiggling on my cock."

She wiggles again. The little vixen. "But it feels big and hard."

"It's what happens when the sexiest woman I've ever met is sitting in my lap."

"There you go again. Saying the right thing at the right time," she says as she rubs her core up and down my cock.

"Something you need, firecracker?"

"You. I need you."

"How do you want me?"

"With less clothes on."

Thank fuck. I'm about to come in my jeans and all she's done is rub herself up and down me.

"Trust me?" I ask. At her nod, I grasp her hips and roll her onto her back. I unsnap her jeans. "This okay?" I ask with my hand on her zipper.

"More than okay."

I don't waste any time. I drag her jeans and underwear down her legs and throw the material over my shoulder. Her core is now exposed to me and I want to taste her. My mouth waters at the idea. But I doubt my little firecracker is ready for me to bury my nose in her pussy. Next time.

"You want on top?" I ask.

"Yes, please."

I pull my wallet out of my back pocket and dig out a condom before rolling to my back. I start to unzip my jeans but Leia slaps my hands away.

"My turn."

"Have at it."

She unzips me and I lift my hips for her to lower my jeans. My cock pops out and her mouth gapes open.

"Holy shit."

My cock twitches at her compliment and her eyes widen.

"Maybe this isn't a good idea after all."

"Hey." I cradle her face and lift her head to meet my gaze. "We don't have to do this if you don't want to."

She licks her lips as her eyes zero in on my cock. "I want to. I'm not sure…."

"If you're not sure, we'll stop." I'll need to hurry to the bathroom to jack off before I explode, but we'll stop. I would never pressure a woman into having sex with me.

"I'm sure about having sex. I'm not sure that monster will fit into me."

"It'll fit. I need to make you ready first, though."

"I'm more than ready to have an orgasm that isn't self-induced."

"Trust me." It's not a question this time but she still nods.

I roll her to her back and cover her with my body. I meld my lips to hers. She immediately opens and I thrust my tongue inside. I explore her mouth until her fingers dig into my shoulders. Once I know she's fully on board, I draw my hand down her body until I reach her core.

I spread her lips and find her clit. I rub circles around it and she widens her legs with a moan. I move my hand lower to her pussy and spear her with two fingers. She's hot and wet. My cock twitches in response.

"You're so wet," I say against her lips.

"Your fault."

I've barely touched her and she's soaked. She's so responsive to me.

I could play with her pussy all day long but my cock is impatient. It's been five long years since it's been buried in a woman.

I get to my knees and don the condom. "You certain about this?"

"Certain I'm going to knee you in the gonads if you don't get on with it."

"There's my little firecracker." I tap her thigh. "Spread your legs."

She widens her legs until I can see her excitement leaking from her pussy. I squeeze the base of my cock to stop from getting too excited before I manage to bury myself in her.

I settle myself between her thighs and hitch my cock at her entrance. I glance down and realize I forgot to remove her shirt. But I'm not stopping now. Not unless she wants me to.

I meet her gaze as I sink my cock inch by inch into her. Her eyes widen and her mouth drops open. I stop to let her adjust to my size, but she slaps my bicep. "Don't you dare stop now."

I continue to bury myself in her until I bottom out and my balls slap against her ass. Her walls spasm around me and I grit my teeth before I come. I'm not some one-pump wonder. I want to show her how good we can be together. How much pleasure I can give her.

Her back arches and she winds her legs around my hips. "More."

I can give her more. I ease out before sinking back into her again.

"Faster."

I thrust into her faster this time and her nails dig into my shoulders as she hisses, "Yes."

I grit my teeth as her walls tighten around me. "You're so tight. I don't think I'll last long."

"Harder."

Her wish is my command. I increase my pace until I'm pounding into her. My little firecracker is with me every step of the way. She digs her heels into my ass and arches into me with every thrust.

"I-I-I…"

Her walls squeeze me. "Come, Leia. Come all over my cock."

"Fender!" she screams as her walls clamp down on mine.

I continue to thrust into her as she rides out her orgasm. I wait until she sighs before I allow myself to lose myself in her body.

I only need a few strokes before my climax hits.

"Leia," I groan as my rhythm fails me and I ride my own high.

I collapse on her but roll to my side before I squash her as I try to catch my breath.

"Wow. Just wow. I wouldn't have waited nine years to have sex again if I had known how awesome it can be."

"Only awesome with me, firecracker," I grumble.

I'm not talking smack. Sex has never been this good for me.

I plan to spend as much time as possible buried inside of Leia in the future. One taste was not enough. I doubt I will ever get enough of her.

Chapter 21

Daddy – a word that causes fear in men and women alike

LEIA

The sun flutters against my face and I groan. Ugh. I forgot to shut the curtains before I went to bed last night. I roll away from the sun and slam smack dab into a hard wall. A hard wall of muscles to be exact.

"Good morning, firecracker," Fender greets.

Memories of the previous night assault me. Realizing how much I enjoy being a full participant during sex. Exploring those muscles I've been drooling over ever since he moved in next door. Discovering he has a full chest of tattoos and licking every single one of them.

"Good morning," I croak. I clear my throat and try again. "Good morning."

He kisses my nose. "How are you feeling?"

Freaking fabulous, I think but refuse to say out loud. No reason to inflate the rockstar's ego. "Good."

He tucks a strand of hair behind my ear. "Good is okay. But I can make you feel great."

That he can. That he can.

"You can?" I cock an eyebrow in challenge.

"You don't believe me? Do you need a demonstration?"

"I believe I do need a demonstration."

He growls before rolling me onto my back and crawling on top of me. "I can demonstrate." He focuses on my lips and I bite my bottom one. His mouth is nearly on mine before I remember – morning breath.

"Eek!" I shove a hand in front of my mouth.

"What's wrong?"

"Morning breath."

"I don't give a shit about morning breath."

"I do." In fact, I should probably brush my hair along with my teeth. Maybe jump in the shower while I'm at it.

"Okay." He nuzzles my neck. "No kissing." He lifts his head to wink at me. "On the mouth."

Oh my. I squirm as I imagine how his beard would feel scraping against my thighs as his mouth works me.

He crawls down my body and fits his shoulders between my legs. He nibbles along my thigh until he reaches my core where he rubs his nose along the crotch of my panties. Why am I wearing underwear? Why did I insist on putting on clothes in the middle of the night?

"Mom, I'm home," Isla shouts before the front door slams. Ah yes, now I remember why I refused to sleep naked.

"Good morning!" I shout back to stop her from coming to find me.

"Where are you?" So much for her not searching for me.

"I'll be out in a minute."

My bedroom door squeaks open and I throw the blankets over Fender. I feel his body tremble with his laughter and I kick him for good measure.

"There you are!" Isla bounces into the room. "Why are you still in bed?"

"Just being lazy."

"Oh, can I be lazy, too?" She starts to jump on the bed.

"No!" She jerks and her eyes widen at me. I clear my throat. "I mean I should be getting up."

She frowns. "Okay. Can I have pancakes for breakfast?"

I normally don't allow pancakes for breakfast except on special occasions, but I'm desperate for her to leave before she realizes what I'm hiding under the covers. "Yep. I'll be out in a minute."

She skips toward the hallway. "Shut the door on your way out."

"You're being weird today," she says as she shuts the door.

Once the door is closed, I whip the covers off Fender who bursts into laughter. I slam a hand over his mouth.

"Shush. She'll hear you."

He shrugs. "She'll figure out I'm here when I walk out of the room anyway."

"You're cute. You think you're walking out the door." I point to the window.

"I'll crawl out the window but I am having pancakes for breakfast."

"Deal." I push him out of the bed. "Now get moving."

"Can I get dressed first?"

I pick his clothes off of the floor and throw them at him. "Stop stalling, grumpapottamus."

"I prefer King of the Grumps."

I roll my eyes. "Of course, you do."

He dresses and I sigh as he hides all those delicious muscles. Those delicious tattoos I'm slowly becoming obsessed with.

He palms my neck and kisses my forehead. "Stop staring at me like you want to eat me or I'll never be able to zip my jeans."

I glance down and notice he's hard.

"I really hate having a child right now."

He squeezes my neck. "No, you don't."

It's true. I don't. But I do wish her sleepover had lasted longer.

I push up on my tiptoes and kiss him briefly before pulling away to steer him toward the window. He grunts as I open it. He probably thinks I'm crazy but I'm not ready for my kid to know I had sex.

Once Fender's gone, I rush through my morning ritual knowing he won't wait long before barging into the house.

"Who wants pancakes?" I ask Isla when I enter the kitchen.

"Me," Fender answers as he opens the backdoor.

Isla's nose wrinkles. "Why are you coming through the backdoor? Did Mom kick you out? Was she mad at you?"

Fender raises an eyebrow my way.

"What do you mean?" I hedge.

Isla rolls her eyes. "He stayed overnight."

I groan. So much for her not knowing I had sex. I fear another conversation about what adults do when they like each other is approaching.

"He did?"

"Mom," she huffs. "He was in your bed. Are you mad at him?"

"I'm not mad at him," I claim although I'm a little irritated with the know-it-all look Fender's got going on his face at the moment.

"Good. Because I like Fender."

He ruffles her hair. "I like you, too, cutie pie."

"Did you have fun at the sleepover?" I ask because I am done discussing where Fender slept last night.

"It was okay. After Storm got sick, they took our candy away."

I bite my tongue before I say good. "What did you do? Watch movies? Play games?"

"Yeah."

She pats the chair next to her. "Sit down here, Fender."

"Maybe your mom needs help making the pancakes."

I lift the box of pancake mix. "All fine here. Go ahead and relax."

He sits next to my daughter and she smiles up at him. "Does this mean you're my new daddy now?"

I gasp and drop the pan onto the stove with a thump. "What?"

"Storm said if a man stays over night with your mom, he's your new daddy."

My gaze meets Fender's. Panic is clear to see in his eyes. The same panic is coursing through my body. I could barely agree to date Fender. I'm not ready for a full-on relationship with him.

And, considering he's panicking as hard as I am, Fender obviously isn't ready for one either. Disappointment kicks me in the stomach. Why do I feel disappointed? I literally just thought I'm not ready for a full-on relationship with him.

"Did I say the wrong thing?" Isla glances back and forth between us.

"Maybe I should go." Fender starts for the door. "We'll talk later."

"Is he mad at me?" Isla asks when the door shuts behind him.

"Of course not, honey."

"But he was happy before I asked him about being my daddy." Her bottom lip trembles and I rush to her.

"It's okay. Everything's okay," I reassure her.

"He hates me!" she screams and promptly bursts into tears.

I pull her into my arms and rock her back and forth. "Fender doesn't hate you."

"He doesn't want to be my dad," she wails.

This is why I don't date. This is why I don't trust men. They flee at the first hurdle and leave you all alone to deal with the aftermath.

Stupid men. I shouldn't have asked Fender inside yesterday.

Lesson learned. No more men. And, this time, I'm sticking to it.

Chapter 22

Ice cream – the yummiest of distractions

LEIA

I'm about done with Isla moping around the house. And I'm beyond pissed at Fender. He doesn't want a relationship with me? Fine. But he can't cut my child out of his life with a snap of his fingers. I won't let him.

Time for a distraction. "Why don't we go for some ice cream?"

"Ice cream?"

The tiny thread of excitement in Isla's voice is enough for me. "Get your shoes on. Let's go."

"But we haven't had dinner yet."

"We're making an exception today."

"Okay." She shrugs and goes to find her shoes. So much for ice cream cheering her up.

I wrap my arm around her shoulders as we walk toward Main Street. Main Street in Winter Falls is adorable. It's lined with small, unique mom-and-pop stores you won't find in a suburban mall such as a candle store that sells sexy candles, a bookstore specialized in smutty books, and a small grocery store that accepts barter instead of cash.

It's also completely safe for pedestrians – and kids who don't pay enough attention to where they're going – since most cars are banned. Except electric cars like the one Fender has.

Fender. I swallow my irritation with the man. My daughter needs my attention now not some fickle man who flees at the first bump in the road.

We reach *Unleashed,* the pet store, and Isla tugs on my hand. "Can we go in? Can we?"

I usually stay far away from pet stores considering my daughter's been begging me for a puppy since she was old enough to say the word. As if I have time to care for another living thing.

"Okay," I say now since I can't deny her when her eyes are still red from crying most of the day.

"Good afternoon, Wilson family," a man greets when we enter. I'm starting to think the residents of Winter Falls were given a briefing with all of our essential information before our arrival considering everyone seems to know our names. "I'm Forest."

"Forest?" Isla giggles. "You have a silly name."

"Isla," I warn. "We don't judge."

"Isla is correct. My name is kind of silly."

"I think it's cool," I say to make up for my daughter being all judgy-face.

"Are you an animal lover?" Forests asks Isla who's gazing around the store.

"I want a puppy."

"I'm afraid I don't have any puppies at the moment." Her shoulders slump. "But I do have a squirrel. Do you want to meet Sammy?"

"Yes!" She bounces on her toes.

He leads her to a large cage where a squirrel is chirping away while scurrying around.

"She's cute. Can I hold her?" Isla asks.

"I'm afraid not. But you can give her a nut."

Isla nabs the nut from Forest and holds it out to Sammy the squirrel. Sammy doesn't hesitate to steal the nut from my daughter's hands.

At the sound of her giggle, relief hits me. Isla is a wonderful little girl but she is prone to spending the day sulking if she doesn't get what she wants.

"You ready for some ice cream?" I ask after Isla's spent a good ten minutes watching the squirrel.

I don't wait for her answer and herd her out of the pet store to the ice cream store, *Feather's Frozen Delights,* next door.

"Isla and Leia, two of my favorite people," Feather greets as we enter.

"I'm getting ice cream," Isla declares in response.

Feather motions to the counter. "Good thing I have ice cream then." She grabs a cone and a scoop. "What's your favorite flavor?"

"Strawberry!"

She prepares Isla's cone before addressing me. "What'll it be, Leia?"

"I'll have blackberry, please."

"Good choice. As is Fender. He's…"

I slash a hand in front of my throat to cut her off. Feather's nose wrinkles in confusion. I point to Isla and mouth *they had a fight.* It's not exactly the truth, but it's the easiest and quickest way to stop this gossip gal from starting her matchmaking magic.

"This ice cream is fabulous," I say before Feather can figure out how to proceed. I pay and then motion to the door. "Do you want to sit in the gazebo?"

Isla shrugs and I hurry her out the door. We pass *Clove's Coffee Corner* on our way to the town square but the café has already closed for the day. Phew. I don't need another gossip gal bringing up Fender.

We settle on a bench in the gazebo situated on the town square. This town may be full of quirky residents but the view is worth it. Mountains rise up looking all majestic in the distance. I could stare at the view all day.

Winter Falls is everything I ever wanted for my child. And worth every sacrifice I had to make to get here. I love this town and its inhabitants. Except for the neighbor who is currently on my shit list. Speaking of which.

"Isla," I begin.

"Mom," she whines.

"What?" All I did was say her name.

"You're using the lecture voice."

"I don't have a lecture voice."

She snorts. "Yes, you do. Isla, do you know what happens if you don't clean your room? Isla, do you want us to have ants because you didn't do the dishes?"

"I don't sound..." I trail off. I can't win an argument with Isla this way.

"Isla," I begin again.

"Still the lecture voice," she mutters.

"Maybe it's time for a lecture."

"Whatever. I knew there was a hitch."

"A hitch?"

She lifts her ice cream. "You never allow ice cream before dinner."

She makes me out as a hard ass parent. She thinks I'm a hard ass? She should meet my parents. Talk about hard asses. My rules are a joke compared to theirs.

I couldn't go out during the school week except for school activities. I wasn't allowed to phone friends during the week. I couldn't have an afternoon snack unless I finished my homework first. And the lecture if I didn't get good grades? I shiver at the memory.

But Isla will never meet her grandparents because they refuse to acknowledge her existence. My heart aches at the reminder of how easily my parents threw us away.

I rub a hand over my chest and force those memories into the box I built especially for them. Just to be certain I put a padlock on the box as well.

"I want to discuss Fender."

Her bottom lip wobbles and I nearly cave. But I can't. I'm a parent. I have to do the hard things because if I don't, no one else will.

"There's no reason to be upset."

"He doesn't like me," she whines.

"Fender likes you."

"He ran out of the house."

Thanks for the reminder, kid. "He wasn't running from you. He was running from me."

Her little nose wrinkles. "Huh?"

"Here's the thing. You and me?" I motion between the two of us. "We're a unit. We're a family."

"Yeah, you're my mom."

"But people don't treat us as a family. They treat us as two individual people. Do you understand?"

"Yeah?"

I try again. "What I mean is that you have one relationship with Fender and I have a different relationship with him."

"Okaaay."

"My relationship with Fender doesn't affect yours."

Her brow wrinkles. "I'm confused."

Probably because I'm doing a crappy job of explaining myself. I inhale a deep breath and try again.

"What I'm trying to say is that your relationship with Fender isn't the same as mine."

"Duh."

"Smart alec," I mutter. "He's mad at me, not at you."

"But he got mad about something I said."

"Forget I said mad. He's upset with me because what you said reminded him of something."

"Reminded him of what?"

I don't even have a shovel and I dug myself a hole deep enough to be a ditch to bury myself in.

"Adult stuff."

"Mom," she whines. "You always say adult stuff when you don't want to tell me the truth."

"This time, my little smart alec, I said adult stuff because it's Fender's stuff. Stuff he trusted me to keep private and not tell anyone else."

Stuff she wouldn't understand even if I did tell her.

"Even me?" she asks.

"Even you."

"Huh." She continues to eat her ice cream and I don't speak again. I remain silent and give her the space to let what I said sink in.

"Can I go see the squirrel again?" she asks once she's finished her cone.

"I'm not getting you a puppy," I say as I stand to throw our napkins away.

As we walk to the pet store, I blow out a breath in relief. She's done being upset with Fender for now.

I, on the other hand, plan to give the man a piece of my mind the next time I see him. How dare he make my daughter think he doesn't like her.

Chapter 23

Puppy – the best apology a little girl can ask for

FENDER

My heart pounds as I march up the walkway to Leia's house. I wouldn't blame her if she slammed the door in my face.

But I hope she doesn't. I need to make things right with her and Isla. I should have never fled this morning. Now, Isla thinks I hate her. I heard her scream the words.

I don't hate her. I could never hate her. I love the cutie pie. How can I not? She's perfect.

I knock on Leia's door. She scowls at me when she opens it. But she doesn't say a word. Merely points to Isla sitting in the living room.

I make my way to the little girl. I set the box with her gift on the floor before sitting on the coffee table in front of her.

"Hey, Isla."

She narrows her eyes at me and crosses her arms over her chest. She couldn't resemble her mother more if she tried. She's adorable.

"I need to apologize."

She nods.

"I'm sorry I ran away this morning."

She doesn't immediately accept my apology. Not my mini-firecracker.

"Why did you run away?"

Darn. She isn't going to make this easy for me.

"My reasons have nothing to do with you."

She sighs. "Mom said the same thing. You have adult reasons."

"I do have my reasons, but it doesn't excuse me running away like a bear caught with his hand in a honey jar."

She giggles the way I hoped she would.

"Do you accept my apology?"

She studies me. "Will you run away again?"

Tough crowd. "I'll try not to." I pat her thigh. "But no matter what happens, please remember it's not your fault. There's nothing wrong with you. You're perfect."

Leia snorts from behind me. "A perfect pain in my behind," she mutters.

"Do you accept my apology?" I ask Isla again.

"As long as you don't run away again."

I hold out my hand. "I promise," I vow as we shake. "I'm glad you accepted my apology because I have a present for you."

Isla's eyes widen as I pick up the box and set it on the table. "What is it?"

I stand and motion to the box. "Open it and find out."

She jumps to her feet and rips the box open. When she sees what's inside, her bottom lip trembles. "For me?"

"For you." I reach inside and pick up the puppy before placing her in Isla's arms.

"She's mine?" The excitement in her eyes as she asks the question makes me want to buy her a dozen puppies.

"She's yours."

"I have a puppy!" she squeals.

I ruffle her hair. "You have a puppy."

"She's pretty." She plops to the floor with the puppy in her arms. "Hi, puppy," she whispers. "We're going to be best friends." Her happiness is worth every second of anxiety and fear I went through today.

"A word?" Leia doesn't wait for me to answer. She drags me into the kitchen.

"What the hell, Fender?" she hisses.

My brow furrows. "What's wrong?"

"What's wrong? What's wrong?" She clenches her jaw and a vein in her forehead pulses. My little firecracker is pissed off. "What's wrong is you bought my daughter a puppy without asking me first."

Oh shit. "I didn't think."

Her nostrils flare. "Obviously not."

"I should have asked you first."

"Damn straight you should have. I'm her mother. You don't give a child a living animal without consulting her mother first."

"I'm sorry." I want to offer to return the puppy but I can't. Isla's face lit up when she first held the dog. I'm not taking it away from her.

"You can't simply throw money at a problem because you're rich."

"I'm not throwing money at a problem. I knew Isla wanted a puppy and I got her one."

"Without asking me first. Do you know how much extra work a puppy is? She has to be potty trained. And until she is, someone has to clean up her messes."

"I'll clean up her messes."

Her eyes widen in disbelief. "You? The big, bad rockstar is going to clean up puppy pee and poop."

"I can clean." I'm not a spoiled brat.

"When I call you at three in the morning, you're going to rush over here with cleaning supplies in hand and clean up the puppy's mess?"

"I prefer to leave the cleaning supplies here."

She ignores me to continue her rant, "And once the little furball is potty trained, she needs to be walked several times a day. You gonna do those walks, too?"

I shrug. "Sure."

"What about when you're on tour? Or recording? Or – how about this – when you leave Winter Falls for good?"

"I don't have any plans to leave." Especially not if she's here.

Her nostrils flare and her eyes narrow. "Charles didn't have any plans to leave either."

I palm her neck and draw her near. "I am not that asshole. Did I fuck up this morning? Yeah, I did. I admit it." I squeeze her neck. "I see those wheels turning in your head. You think I ran away from you this morning."

"I was there. You did run away from me."

"I didn't run away from you."

"I get it, already. You don't want a relationship."

"Wrong. I wouldn't have asked you out if I didn't want a relationship."

"You said you could only offer me a one-night stand."

"That was then. This is now."

"But—"

"I screwed up this morning. I admit it. Isla's question about becoming her dad reminded me of everything I thought I had with Vicki and everything she tore away and I lost it. But I promise you, it won't happen again."

She raises her eyebrows in disbelief. "You said all women betray you."

"And you pointed out what an asshat I was to think that."

"It is pretty stupid to paint all women with the same brush."

But it's okay for her to paint all men with the same brush because of how her parents and Isla's dad abandoned her? Someone's being a hypocrite but – despite my actions this morning – I'm not a stupid man.

Instead of telling her, I'll show her she can rely on me, unlike the men in her past.

"I promise I'll do my best not to let my past ruin my future."

She gasps and tries to retreat a step. "Future?"

Who's running now?

"Future," I insist.

Her eyes dart around as if seeking an escape but she blows out a breath and straightens her back. There's my firecracker.

"We can take it day by day," I offer.

"Okay." She nods. "Day by day."

She appears relieved and I don't push her despite knowing I want a future with her. I can give her time to adjust to our new status.

"Mom!" Isla yells, and Leia runs to her without a backward glance. It's cute how she thinks she can run away from me.

"The puppy had an accident," Isla announces when we arrive in the living room.

Leia glares at me. I hold up my hands. "I'll get the cleaning supplies."

I quickly gather what I need and clean up the mess.

"Shall we take her for a walk?" I ask once I finish. "She might need to go out."

"Do you have a leash for her? Poop bags? A bed?" Leia throws questions at me. Judging by the twinkle in her eye, she thinks she's caught me. Wrong, my little firecracker.

"I bought all the supplies." Somone at the pet store in White Bridge made a very nice commission today. "There's a box on your porch with everything in it. I'll get it."

I set the box of supplies in the hallway and dig out the leash.

Leia giggles when she sees it. "You bought a pink, sparkly leash?"

I shrug. "I thought Isla would like it."

Isla screeches as she snatches the leash from me. "I love it!"

I show her how to attach the leash to the harness before we go outside for our first walk with the puppy.

"Come on, puppy. Come on," Isla urges the dog forward.

"You need to name her," I say.

Isla's eyes widen. "I get to name her?"

"She's your dog."

"Can I name her Princess?"

"You can name her anything you want."

"I think she's a princess."

"Then, her name's Princess."

"Come on, Princess." The puppy perks up at the name as if she recognizes it.

"What kind of dog is she?" Isla asks as we begin down the sidewalk.

"She's a rescue. As near as the shelter could tell she's a cross between a chihuahua and a dachshund."

Her nose wrinkles. "What's a dachshund?"

"I'll show you a picture on my phone when we're back home."

Home. For the first time in my life, the word means something more than a place to sleep. It's where my heart is. Home is where these two are. I can't imagine my life without them.

I love Isla and I'm falling for her mom. I wrap an arm around Leia's shoulders and draw her near while Isla runs in front of us giggling with her puppy.

This is it. This is what I've been looking for. I messed up today, but I won't mess up again. I'm not letting these two go.

Sage waves from her front porch. "Aren't you a lovely family?"

"We're not a family!" Leia shouts back.

Maybe not yet, firecracker. But I'll do everything in my power to make us one.

Chapter 24

Get it – when you realize why women throw their panties at rockstars

LEIA

"Do you want to call and check on Isla?" Fender asks as we walk to *Electric Vibes,* the one and only bar in Winter Falls.

We just finished dinner at the *Naked Falls Brewery* with Indigo and Virginia and his bandmates and are off to the bar for a few drinks. I'm excited since I haven't had a chance to visit the bar yet. I heard it's a hippie haven.

I check my phone. "She hasn't messaged and I don't have any missed calls. She's probably fine."

She's staying overnight at her friend Storm's house. I spoke to Honor when I dropped her off and I feel confident my daughter's in good hands.

"I don't mind," Fender says.

I study his face. Worry lines bracket his eyes. "Do you want to call and check up on her?"

He shrugs. "It wouldn't hurt. The last time she was away for the night, she got sick."

She didn't get sick, Storm did, but I don't correct him. Not when it's obvious he's worried about my daughter. Butterflies flutter with excitement in my stomach at his show of concern. I've waited a long time for someone to share the burden of raising a child with.

He's not sharing the burden, I remind myself. He's temporary.

Liar. Liar. Pants on fire.

I ignore my inner voice and dial Isla's number.

"I'm fine, Mom," she answers.

"Well, hello to you, too," I greet and then throw Fender under the bus. "Fender wants to say hi."

He snatches the phone from me. "Having fun, cutie pie?"

I can't hear her answer but the smile on his face is enough for me. My ovaries nearly explode at those dimples appearing for my daughter.

Let's make a baby with him.

My inner voice must be high. I am not going to have a baby with this man. I'm not ready to have a serious relationship with him. A baby isn't a possibility.

Need I remind you of the liar, liar pants on fire situation?

I ignore my obviously drunk inner voice as Fender ends the call and hands me my phone.

"Satisfied?"

Before he has a chance to answer, Gibson pushes his way in between us. "Who were you calling cutie pie? Are you two in a throuple? Can I join?" He waggles his eyebrows. "I promise not to behave."

Fender slaps a hand on Gibson's face and pushes him away. "No."

Gibson juts out his bottom lip. "But I'm fun. I promise I'm fun."

Before I can tell Gibson I don't fall for pouting, a woman screeches, "I don't care, Uncle Mercury." She's standing in front of the bar blocking Old Man Mercury from the entrance.

"Get out of my way, Mercy," he grumbles at her.

"No. You shouldn't be drinking."

"I'll drink if I damn well want to."

"The doctor said—"

"I don't give a shit what the doctor said."

Gibson strolls up to them. "If the man wants a drink, let him drink."

Mercy glares at him. If she could spit fire from her eyes, he would be a pile of ashes. "I don't recall asking for your opinion. In fact, I don't know who you are."

"Gibson Lewis." He bows. "At your service."

"Whatever." She turns away from him to face Old Man Mercury again. "Uncle Mercury, you said—"

He wags a finger at her. "No, I didn't. You assumed."

"Excuse me." Gibson stands in front of Mercy. "Do you not know who I am?"

Mercy plants her hands on her hips. "Do you not see I'm busy?"

"She's awesome," Indigo declares. "She's going to be my next bestie."

"Lucky woman," I mutter.

"Leia Wilson, don't you use your sarcastic tone with me. You love me and you know it."

"Against my will."

"I'm with Leia," Virginia says. "Leave the woman be."

Indigo laughs. "You're hilarious."

Jett snags Gibson's wrist and draws him away from the woman. "Try to accept your defeat with some grace."

Gibson's eyes are the size of saucers as he stares at Mercy. "She didn't know who I was."

Fender wraps an arm around my shoulder. "Shall we go inside?"

"I'm with Fender," Dylan says as he clasps Virginia's hand. "Those two could argue about whether it's dark outside or not for an hour nonstop."

"You aren't going to stop them?" Virginia asks.

"I'm off duty."

Cash leads Indigo to the bar. At the door, Indigo stops to wave at Mercy. "See you later."

Mercy stares at Indigo. She's probably wondering if Indigo has lost her mind. I get it. I've wondered the same thing many times myself.

My mouth gapes open when we enter the bar. "It is a hippie haven."

The walls are covered with memorabilia from the hippie age – posters of Janis Joplin, Joni Mitchell, and Jimi Hendrix to name a few. The chairs and tables are a mishmash with none matching each other. And the lightbulbs are all different colors giving the entire room a psychedelic feel.

"Cool, isn't it?" Fender has to shout to be heard above the music blaring from the old-fashioned jukebox.

"I can't believe I haven't been in here before."

"We'll come more often," he says as if it's the most natural thing in the world for the two of us to be together. I'm not convinced yet.

The band gathers at a table in the corner where it's less noisy. A woman arrives and slams a pitcher of beer on the table. "I don't want any fights."

"We don't fight in bars," Dylan claims.

"Anymore," Cash adds.

"We also didn't order this beer," Jett says.

Gibson elbows him. "It's free beer."

"You don't know it's free."

"Actually," the waitress interrupts. "It is free. I'm Cassandra, the owner of this joint. You can have as many drinks as you want for free under one condition."

Gibson raises his hand. "I volunteer as tribute. I can rock your world."

"I'll let my husband know." She nods toward a man who appears to be a lumberjack sitting at the bar.

Dylan slaps a hand over Gibson's mouth. "Ignore him. We all do."

"What's the condition?" Cash asks.

"You play a set." She indicates the small stage where the instruments are already set up.

"Do the girls get free drinks, too?" Indigo asks. "Or just the band?"

Cassandra points to Indigo, Virginia, and me. "You three get free drinks. The other women in the bar who big mouth wants to seduce? No."

"I prefer the word charm," Gibson says.

Cassandra ignores him. "What do you want?" she asks Indigo.

"A porn star martini."

"I'll have one, too." I've always wanted to try a martini, but my usual lifestyle doesn't exactly scream cocktails.

As soon as Cassandra's gone, Fender leans over to whisper in my ear, "Don't drink too much. I have plans for us tonight."

"I've never had drunken sex before."

He smirks. "Then, have at it, firecracker. I'm happy to be your first."

"Who's ready to rock this town?" Cash shouts as he lifts his beer.

Fender frowns. "I'm not playing. Leia and I are on a date."

Jett sighs. "Is this how it's going to be from now on since the three of you are in love?" He nearly chokes on the word 'love'.

I push Fender. "Go ahead and play."

He glares at Jett. "Don't listen to the asshole."

"Seriously, it's fine. Virginia and Indigo are here."

"I'm her bestie," Indigo declares.

Fender ignores her to ask me, "You sure?"

"I'm sure."

He studies my face for a second before nodding. "Okay, I'll play."

The five band members down their beers in one go before standing and approaching the stage. The crowd begins to cheer. "Sinners! Sinners! Sinners!"

"Have you ever heard Fender play live before?" Indigo asks. I shake my head. "You're in for a treat."

Our martinis arrive and I sip on mine while I watch Fender get ready to play. After a few minutes, he nods at Cash.

"Good evening, Winter Falls!" Cash shouts as if he's greeting a stadium of fans and not a group of people in a small town. "We've got a new song for you tonight."

Indigo squeals and jumps out of her chair. She grabs my hand and pulls.

"I'm good."

"You are not sitting in the corner while your boyfriend plays on stage."

"Not my boyfriend."

She rolls her eyes. "You keep telling yourself that."

"Come on." Virginia nudges me. "She won't give up until all of us are in front of the stage."

"Dog with a bone," I mutter as I stand and follow her.

Fender notices me and winks. If rock gods were a thing, he'd be one with his bass in his hands, his biceps flexed, and his strong legs planted wide. Too bad he's not shirtless with his tattoos on display.

"We've got a new song for you tonight," Cash declares and nods to Jett who drums a beat to start them off.

Cash begins to sing.

I've been searching for a place to call my own;

Where the winds of change have never blown;
Yearning for a place to finally call home;
I'm gonna find that place to settle down;
Where the stars above never let me frown;
With every hardship faced;
I'll carve my own space;
I've found my haven where I belong;
With her in my arms, I can't be wrong.

Cash repeats the final lyric and Fender's gaze finds mine. He stares into my eyes as he mouths the words. *With you in my arms, I can't be wrong.*

My heart squeezes and I clutch my chest. I want to be the one in his arms. Always. Oh no. I'm falling for Fender. How did this happen? Yesterday I wasn't ready for a serious relationship and today I'm falling in love.

Indigo elbows me and I'm thankful for the interruption from my thoughts. "Now you get it."

"Get what?" I shout back to be heard.

"Why women throw their panties at rockstars."

No one better throw their panties at Fender. I'll eviscerate them before forcing them to eat their intestines. And they won't be getting any ketchup either.

Fender's mine.

Chapter 25

Firecracker and vixen – are not mutually exclusive

FENDER

We play five songs before calling it quits. Although Leia appears to be having a good time with Indigo and Virginia, I'm glad when I'm off the stage and she's in my arms again.

"You want another martini?" I ask.

"I'm good."

I notice Cash grab his girl and head out. Dylan and Virginia follow them. Good idea.

"You want to stay or are you ready to go home?" I shout in Leia's ear since the crowd is still clamoring for an encore.

"I'm ready to go."

I wave to Gibson and Jett before leading Leia to the exit. "You okay to walk?"

"It's less than five minutes."

I tweak her nose. "Not an answer."

"Let's walk."

I wrap my arm around her waist and she cuddles close to me as we start toward her house.

"I love this town," she says on a sigh.

"Agree."

"I don't miss the ocean at all." She waves toward the mountains in the distance. "Those more than make up for a bunch of salt water."

"You don't miss the city?"

"And miss having a pet store that sells squirrels and a candle store that sells sexy candles?"

"Wouldn't want to miss those."

"Although it does kind of freak me out how the woman who makes the sex candles is old enough to be my grandmother. I actually think my grandmother was younger than her when she passed away."

"Petal is a character."

"All of the gossip gals are."

I grunt in agreement.

"Should we go pick up Princess?" she asks when we're nearly at her house.

"Princess is fine. The woman she's with manages the wildlife refuge."

"I can't believe you asked the wife of a movie star to puppysit my dog."

I shrug. "Movie stars are people, too."

And fame is an illusion. It can disappear at the snap of your fingers.

She unlocks the door before looking up at me. "Do you want to come in?"

My cock twitches. He's ready.

"Are you sure?" I ask, although I'm already entering the house.

Leia doesn't answer. She takes my hand and leads me down the hallway to her bedroom.

I wrap my arms around her and walk her backwards until the back of her knees hit the bed. "You're not drunk."

"I only had one martini."

"I thought you wanted to experience drunk sex."

She bites her bottom lip. "I don't know if I'm ready for drunk sex."

I pull her lip away from her teeth. "There's no rush. I won't pressure you."

"You're not pressuring me."

I press my hard cock against her belly. "Good, because I have plans for us tonight."

Her eyes flare in response. "Plans?" she pants.

I rub my nose along hers. "Naked plans."

Her breath hitches and her breasts rub against my chest. Not good enough. I want to feel her naked skin against mine.

"May I?" I reach for the hem of her shirt. At her nod, I lift the material up and over her head to reveal her breasts straining at her red, lacy bra.

I trail my finger along the edge of the lace. "Is this for me?"

"Maybe it's for me. Maybe it makes me feel sexy."

"You are sexy, firecracker."

I yank the cup of the bra down to reveal her pink nipples. I rub a circle around the areola. Leia moans and her head falls back.

She's the sexiest thing I've ever seen in my life with her face flushed in excitement, her chest jutted forward, her breast spilling out of one bra cup. My cock strains against my zipper. He wants in on the fun.

I reach around Leia and unhook her bra. The lacy material falls to the floor and my hands begin to knead and squeeze her breasts.

"You're torturing me," she complains.

"Patience," I demand but I do drop to my knees and unsnap her jeans before dragging the zipper down to reveal her panties match her bra. I'm glad I didn't know she was wearing this sexy underwear while we were at the bar. I would have embarrassed myself.

She kicks off her sandals and I draw her jeans and panties down her legs. Goosebumps arise on her smooth skin. Damn. I love how responsive she is to my touch.

I stand before grasping her by the hips to lay her down on the bed. Her eyes pop open and I wink before removing my t-shirt. I toe off my shoes before pushing my jeans down my legs.

Leia licks her lips as her eyes rove over my body.

"Like what you see?"

She rolls her eyes. "You know you're sexy."

I flex my bicep and she giggles.

"Are you going to do a workout or get on this bed and finish what you started?"

My cock bobs forward as if to lunge for her. I know what his vote is. I kneel on the bed, and she widens her legs in invitation.

I grin. Her shyness the first time was adorable but a woman who knows what they want and asks for it is sexy as hell.

I draw my hands along the smooth skin of her legs up her calves to her thighs until I reach her core. I skim a finger along her lips before reaching her pussy. I groan as liquid leaks out.

"You're soaked."

She squirms. "Well, um."

I pause my movements. "What?"

"It's really hot when you play your bass."

I smirk. My girl gets horny when I play with the band. Good news since I play music with the band often. I can't wait to bring her to a concert.

I plunge two fingers inside her and moan as her walls convulse around me. She wasn't kidding about getting horny.

"Are you ready for me?"

In response, she lifts her knees and drops them to the side to open herself up to me. "What do you think?"

"You're not a firecracker. You're a vixen."

"Why can't I be both? I'm a single mom. I can multi-task."

I blanket her with my body. I'm going to kiss the smirk right off of her face. I slam my lips on hers. She moans and her lemon taste hits me. I think I'm becoming addicted to lemon.

She tilts her head to the side the way I prefer and I dive in deeper. Her tongue duels with mine as her hands move to my shoulders. She holds on tight as I memorize every single inch of her mouth.

She wraps her legs around my waist and I hitch my cock at her entrance.

"Condom," I say against her mouth.

"No need."

I freeze. "No?"

"You don't have to use a condom. I'm on the pill."

I grit my teeth before my cock overrules my head and thrusts into her. I've never had sex without a condom before. Not even with Vicki.

"I should probably get checked first," I manage to say.

She scowls. "You said you haven't had sex in years."

"I haven't."

"Then, what do you want to get checked for? Is there some STD that lies in wait for years only to pop up and say, 'I'm here!' when you have sex?"

I chuckle. I don't know how she does it but my firecracker can make me laugh in any situation.

"If you're sure."

Her eyes narrow on me. "I appreciate you checking in with me but if you ask me one more time if I'm sure, I'm going to—"

I impale her on my cock before she can finish her threat.

"Fuck," I groan. Her warmth surrounding me without a condom feels better than anything I've ever felt before.

"You." I retreat. "Feel." I sink into her. "Like." I retreat again. "Heaven."

Words elude me after that. I can't form any thoughts except how this is the best sex has ever been for me. I don't want to ever leave. I want to remain buried inside my firecracker until we're old and gray.

My back tingles to let me know I can't stay buried inside Leia without exploding soon. I snake a hand between our bodies to find her clit. I rub circles around it until her walls convulse and tighten around me.

"That's it, my sexy firecracker. Come for me."

Her nails dig into my shoulders before she moans, "Fender."

"I'm here, firecracker. Right here."

As she rides her orgasm, I increase my pace until I lose all sense of time and rhythm.

"Leia," I groan as ecstasy hits me and I come into a woman without a barrier for the first time in my life.

I continue to thrust in and out of her until my climax wanes and I collapse on top of her. I quickly roll to my side.

"Amazing," Leia gasps.

"Best sex of my life."

She smacks my chest. "No need to give me flowery compliments. I'm a sure thing for the rest of the night."

Sex with her is without a doubt the best sex I've ever had. I catch her hand and squeeze it. "Only the rest of the night?"

She shrugs. "I have a kid and a puppy you insisted on giving my kid. I make no guarantees."

I smile as I roll to my side to wrap myself around her. "Better get some sleep while I recover then."

I kiss her temple and settle in with a smile on my face. Leia might not be ready to give me guarantees, but I think I might be ready to give her some of my own.

Chapter 26

Maybe means no — a truth all children know

LEIA

Ugh! It's warm. Are we in the middle of another heatwave? I throw my blanket off of me but the blanket doesn't move. Oh wait. It's not a blanket. It's a man. A heavy, naked man.

"Are we wrestling, firecracker?" Fender asks.

"I'm hot."

"I know you are."

I roll my eyes. "Corny."

"Horny," he corrects and presses his hard length into my back.

He woke me up twice in the middle of the night already. "You're insatiable."

He kisses my neck. "Your fault, sexy firecracker."

I roll over until we're chest to chest and throw a leg over his thighs. He groans in response before palming my neck.

"Don't tempt me."

"What's wrong with tempting you?"

"Isla will be here soon. I don't want her to walk in on us again."

Crap. I forgot about my daughter. I push at his shoulders. "You should go."

Fender refuses to budge. "I'm not going anywhere. I'm not letting Isla think I don't love her."

Love her? Did he say he loves my daughter? Before I have a chance to ask, the front door bangs open.

"Mom! I'm home."

Fender kisses my lips. "Get dressed."

He rolls out of bed and puts his jeans on while I remain on the bed frozen. He loves my daughter?

He slaps the mattress. "Dressed," he orders before sauntering away.

The second the door closes on him, my mind comes back online. Shit. Isla's here. The last time Fender spent the night was a shitshow.

I jump out of bed and race to put on some clothes. I sprint out of the bedroom and down the hall to find Fender and Isla sitting together on the sofa.

"Did you have a good time last night, Isla?" Fender asks and I about melt into the floor. He cares about my daughter. Really cares.

"It was fun but …" She trails off with a scowl.

"But what?" he coaxes.

When she doesn't answer, he pushes. "You can tell me. You can trust me."

"But everyone's talking about how *Cash & the Sinners* played at the bar last night and I wasn't there. I want to hear you play."

"You want to hear the band play?"

"Yes! I love your music."

"Don't worry. We'll make it happen."

She frowns at him and bites her bottom lip. "You're not going to run away again the way you did last time you stayed over?"

Fender pats her thigh. "I'm not going to run away."

"Promise?"

He holds up a hand in a Boy Scout salute. "I promise I won't run away from you ever again."

My chest spasms with love for this man. Whoa. Hold on. Love? I love Fender?

Fender? The man who's gentle with my daughter. The man who's shown me more pleasure than I thought possible. The man who actually apologized and owned up to his mistakes. Shit. It's official. I've fallen for the grumpy rockstar.

Now, I really do melt into the floor. My legs go weak and I slide against the wall until my butt hits the floor. I fell for a rockstar.

This is a disaster. He's not in Winter Falls permanently. He'll leave and take my heart with him. I clutch my chest. It'll be much worse than when Charles left me with a baby. I didn't love Charles the way I love Fender.

I love Fender. I breathe deep as my heart gallops while I allow the realization to sink in.

"Can I ask you something?" Isla asks and I remember I'm not alone. I'm in the hallway eavesdropping on my daughter and the man I love.

"You can ask me anything," Fender says.

"You won't get mad?"

"I won't get mad."

"Are you Mommy's boyfriend?"

I hold my breath as I wait for an answer. Just because I recently realized I love the man doesn't mean he has feelings for me.

"I'm Mommy's boyfriend," Fender says and relief washes through me.

"Does she know you're her boyfriend?" Isla asks.

"Nope."

"Are you going to tell her?"

"Nope."

"Can I tell her?"

He ruffles her hair. "Sure."

She jumps off the couch. "Let's go make pancakes."

I scramble to my feet. I back up a bit before ambling forward as if I'm just now walking to the living room and wasn't eavesdropping the entire time.

"You didn't have breakfast at Storm's house?" Fender asks as he stands. He notices me and winks before following my daughter to the kitchen.

"Storm's mom made us pancakes with spinach." Isla feigns retching.

"Spinach is healthy," I say.

"Mom!" Isla leaps into my arms.

I hug her up tight. It isn't often my eleven-year-old offers me a hug without having an ulterior motive.

"Did you have a good time?" I ask once I've forced myself to let her go.

"It was fun. We played flashlight tag. Do you know what flashlight tag is?" I nod. "We should play it when it's dark tonight."

"Maybe," I hedge since it doesn't get dark until it's nearly her bedtime and a round of tag will have her too wound up to sleep.

"Maybe means no. I'll ask Fender."

Fender chuckles. "You can ask me, but my answer will always be the same as your mom's."

"Is this because your mom's boyfriend now?"

I freeze. What do I do? I can't admit to eavesdropping on their conversation. Isla would never let me forget about the time I eavesdropped on her.

"Nope," Fender says. "Your mom knows what's best for you."

I raise an eyebrow. Is he not going to respond to the boyfriend comment?

"But you are her boyfriend, right?" Isla pushes.

Fender grins and those damn dimples pop out. "You know it, cutie pie."

"Guess what, Mom? Fender is your boyfriend."

I cross my arms over my chest and pretend to be irritated. "He is, is he?"

"Yep. He said so."

"Do I get a say in this?"

Her nose wrinkles. "You like him."

"Isla, cutie pie, why don't you get the ingredients ready for the pancakes while I go talk to your mom?" Fender doesn't wait for her response before he nabs my hand and drags me down the hallway toward the bedroom.

As soon as the door is closed behind us, he pushes me up against the wall and frames my face with his hands.

"You're my boyfriend now?"

"I am," he grumbles. "I've slept in this bed with you twice now. I've been inside you without a condom. This is no longer casual."

"Slept? I don't recall much sleeping."

He tilts his head to the side and studies me. "Are you teasing me?"

I shrug. "I may have heard a bit of your conversation with Isla."

"Good. Then, it's time to get some things straight."

"Things straight? Are you going to give me your varsity jacket and ask me to prom?"

"Never lettered in a sport."

My eyes widen. "You never lettered in a sport?"

"No."

"Not even football?"

"Never played football."

"Did you play any sports?"

"Nope. I'm a musician."

"But how?" I motion toward his body, his very fit body. He smirks and I slap him. "Stop smirking. You know what I mean."

"Playing on stage for several hours each night requires stamina." He presses his body against mine. "And you know I have stamina."

Oh boy, do I know. "So, you're my boyfriend?"

"I'm not a boy," he grumbles. "But this is serious. And we're exclusive."

I debate continuing to give him a hard time, but why would I? He's the man I love and he wants a serious relationship with me.

Am I scared? No doubt about it. Worried I'll get hurt? Hell yeah, I am. But I also realize Fender isn't Charles. Charles never cared about Isla the way Fender does. Charles never cared whether I enjoyed sex with him the way Fender does.

You never loved Charles the way you do Fender.

This time I don't fight with my inner voice. She's right and I'm done fighting.

"Okay."

His eyes sparkle and he smiles. "Okay?"

I nod. "Okay."

I get a brief glimpse of those dimples before he melds his mouth to mine. I open up for him and he dives in. He always kisses me as if he can't get enough. As if he's starving for me. It's intoxicating.

I clutch his biceps and wrap a leg around his hips. He grasps my leg and lifts it higher. I circle his waist and he presses his hard length against my core. Desire pours through me. My body doesn't care how we had sex with this man three times last night. It's ready for another round.

"Are you guys going to come out of the bedroom?" Isla shouts through the door.

I yank my lips from Fender's and lean against the wall as I struggle to gather my breath.

"I'm starving," Isla continues.

Damn it. Things were just getting good. "You certain you want to date a single mother?"

He growls. "I thought I just made it clear we're more than dating."

"I'll rephrase. Are you ready to be in a serious, exclusive relationship with a single mom?"

He smiles and his eyes sparkle. "I am, firecracker. I am."

"Alrighty then. Let me down. We need to make Ms. Perfect Timing her second breakfast."

He kisses my nose. "To be continued."

"Promises. Promises," I say as I sashay away.

He slaps my ass. "I always fulfill my promises."

I hope so, Fender Hays. I hope so. Because I'm taking a big risk letting you into my life and my heart. Be gentle with me.

Chapter 27

Fear – when you're scared to lose someone you just realized is precious

FENDER

"Let's go, grumpapottamus," Gibson shouts through my hotel room door.

I ignore him.

Good morning, Firecracker.

Morning? It's nearly noon. Did you fly to Japan and not tell me?

I chuckle as I write back to Leia.

Press thing didn't end until late last night.

Press thing? Is that the official name? Sounds important and serious.

Smartass.

I'll have you know my ass is incredibly smart.

And sexy.

Nope. You aren't allowed to make sexy comments while chatting.

Is this a rule?

Yep.

Okay, then I won't write about how much I love holding your ass in my hands while I ...

Dot. Dot. Dot. What does dot dot dot mean?

No sexy comments. It's your rule.

You're cruel.

I miss you.

I miss you, too, Mr. Grumpy Pants.

My pants are indeed grumpy.

"Fender!" Dylan shouts. "We need to go now."

I need to go.

More press thingies?

I lo..

Delete. Delete. I can't write I love you to Leia. I don't love her.

If I don't love her, why has my only wish this entire week of press crap been to get back to her and Isla? Why can't I stop thinking about her? Why do I feel empty whenever I go to bed alone? Why am I constantly worried if she's working too hard? If she's taking enough breaks? Whether she and Isla are okay?

Shit. I love Leia. My little firecracker is perfect for me. She's straight as an arrow. Doesn't play any stupid games. And the sex is off the charts. She owns my heart.

I miss you.

Miss you, too.

I shove my phone in my back pocket and stroll to the hotel room door. I open it and nearly get a fist in my face.

"Sorry." Cash drops his hand.

"You ready?" Dylan asks.

I grunt.

"Do you think he grunts in response to Leia's questions?" Jett asks.

"I bet he grunts in bed with her."

I wrap my hand around Gibson's throat. "No."

Dylan taps me on the shoulder. "Can you release him before the paps notice?" He nods to where the vultures are waiting for us at the end of the corridor.

I snarl at Gibson before I release him.

He rubs his throat. "Your hands are freakishly strong."

"Or your neck is weak," Jett says.

"My neck is not weak."

Dylan clears his throat. "Maybe you two can stop speaking before I have to haul Fender off of you again?"

Before either one of them can respond, we're spotted.

"Cash! Cash! Cash!"

"Over here, Cash!"

Cash scowls before clearing his throat and smiling. This smile isn't real, though. It's the smile he uses with the press and fans. Not with Indigo or the band.

"Sorry, guys. We're behind schedule," Cash says.

"Thanks to the big guy having phone sex," Gibson mutters and I elbow him hard enough he crashes into the wall.

Jett laughs as he helps Gibson steady himself while Dylan rolls his eyes.

"You can join us for the press conference down the hall," Cash says to the paps knowing damn well none of them were invited to the press conference.

Our security forms a line in front of us and leads us down the hallway to the room where the press is waiting. Aurora steps out of the room and rakes her gaze over us. She scowls at Jett. He waits until her attention is elsewhere before flipping her off.

Those two need to get over their shit already. Aurora is the best personal assistant this band could ask for. If she ends up quitting because of him, I'm going to pop his head like a big, fat zit. And I'm going to enjoy it.

"You ready?" Aurora asks Cash.

"Ready to get this the hell done with and get home."

I feel the same. I never enjoyed this press shit before, but since I've found Leia and Isla, I really hate it. I'd rather spend my time with my girls.

If I have to be away from them, then I want to be playing music. Not talking to the press who are going to write bullshit they make up about us anyway.

Aurora rolls her eyes. "Let's get this over with then." She opens the door and motions for us to enter in front of her.

We file inside and sit at a long table. Our manager, Mike, stands at one end of the table in front of a microphone. We don't see much of him since Aurora handles most of our day to day shit but he'd never miss an opportunity to be in front of the press.

Mike's a good manager, but he's also an attention whore. Too bad for him, he has no musical talent whatsoever. His talent is discovering talent.

"Good morning," he greets the press.

I lean back in my chair and cross my arms over my chest. This is a waste of my time. No one ever asks me questions. Almost all of the questions are for Cash.

"Cash!" one of the reporters shouts. Here we go.

"Are you still off the market?"

Cash dazzles her with a smile. "I will never be on the market again."

"You're breaking fans' hearts."

He shrugs. "Can't help it. I'm in love."

"What about you, Dylan?" another reporter shouts.

"Sorry, darling, I'm off the market, too."

"Is there anyone in the band who's still single?"

Gibson throws his hand in the air. "I'm single." He waggles his eyebrows. "And not interested in settling down."

Jett leans forward to reach the mic. He stares at Aurora as he speaks. "I'm single, too."

Her eyes narrow to slits before she lifts her hand and flips him off. He chuckles in response.

"What about you, Fender?" a different reporter asks.

"What about me?"

"Are you single?"

"Nope."

The noise in the room rises as the reporters pelt me with questions.

"Who's the lucky woman?"

"Or man."

"How long have you been together?"

"Is she famous?"

"How serious is the relationship?"

"Are there wedding bells in your future?"

"Ladies! Gentlemen!" Mike taps the microphone to get their attention. "One question at a time please." He signals to a reporter waving her hand in the air and she jumps to her feet.

"Fender, can you tell us more?"

"About what?" I ask.

"Who is your partner? How serious is it? Do we hear wedding bells?"

I scowl. I'm not telling the press about Leia and Isla. I don't want them assaulted by the paps. Virginia was cornered by them and it nearly ruined her relationship with Dylan.

I can't chance it. Leia was leery enough about dating me and she hasn't yet experienced the bullshit being a partner of a famous person brings with it. I need to make sure she's tethered to me tight before I introduce her into the world of being famous.

"No comment."

"Come on, Fender. Give us something. Her name. Her occupation. Anything!"

"No comment."

"Does she live in Winter Falls?"

My heart skips a beat. Do they know where I'm living? Damnit.

"What? Where's Winter Falls?"

"You recorded your new release there."

"I'm done."

I stand and walk out of the room. The rest of the band is right behind me.

"Don't worry, Fender," Cash says as he types on his phone. "We'll get back to town before they find her."

Aurora bursts through the door. "I spoke to the pilot. He's getting the jet ready now. And the car is waiting for you out the kitchen entrance."

"Thanks," I grumble.

She squeezes my wrist. "Don't worry. I have everything under control."

She snaps her fingers and our security forms a circle around us. They hurry us through the hallway to the employee entrance of the kitchen.

I don't wait for them to open the backdoor and secure the area. I rush through the door and sprint to the waiting vehicle. The rest of the band hurries after me.

"Go!" I urge the driver.

The security team forces the waiting paps out of the way and the vehicle begins to move.

"The jet is fueled and ready to go," Cash says.

"I warned Virginia to stay inside," Dylan adds.

Crap. In my rush to get to Leia, I forgot all about warning her. I dig my phone out and dial her number.

"Fuck," I growl when I get a busy tone. "I can't get hold of Leia."

"I'll ask Indy to go check on her. Let her know what's happening," Cash offers.

"Thanks."

He scowls. "You don't need to thank me." He picks up his phone and turns away to make the call.

"If they put one hand on Isla, I'm going to kill them all," Jett mutters.

"You won't get the chance," I grumble. I will kill anyone who dares to harm either one of my girls.

I just hope we make it back to Winter Falls in time. We have to.

Damnit. I only realized how much I love Leia this morning. I can't lose her already. I won't lose her.

Chapter 28

Shovel – Not to be confused with a baseball bat

LEIA

"Brody," I warn.

He keeps on going as if I hadn't spoken. "And if you could have those spreadsheets done for me by tonight."

"No."

I grip the phone so hard, my hand begins to hurt. I said no to my boss. What am I doing? If he fires me, I'll be out of a job. And a house. I'll have to leave Winter Falls since there aren't many job opportunities in this small town.

"No?"

I open my mouth to backpedal. To tell him I'll work all night if he wants me to. It doesn't matter how I promised Isla we'd watch a movie together since she's been moping around all week with Fender gone. I'll figure something out. I don't need to sleep. I'm a single mom.

"When do you think you can have the work finished?"

I'm quick to answer before he can change his mind. "To-morrow."

"Let's say the day after tomorrow."

I lift the phone away from my ear and check I'm still connected with Brody. My boss isn't reasonable. He doesn't understand the word exists.

"Are you feeling okay?" I ask. "Do you have a fever? Should I send the doctor over to your house?"

He chuckles and I stop scrolling through my phone for the doctor's number.

"I'm fine."

"But you're being reasonable. Brody Bragg isn't reasonable."

"I can be reasonable."

"You can be a pain in my ass is what you can be."

"You remind me of Soleil."

"Thank you," I say since he loves Soleil to the moon and back.

He sighs. "It's come to my attention that you work way more than forty hours a week for me."

"What? Did you suddenly learn how to count?" I tease. Brody Bragg is a certified genius. He knows how to count.

"Maybe someone made me aware of how demanding I am."

"Soleil strikes again." I write myself a note to send her a gift basket.

"Not Soleil."

If not the mother of his child, then who could possibly… Damn it! There's only one person who would have talked to Brody about how much I work.

"I'm going to kill Fender when he returns."

"I find pranking is more effective. Do you need some tips? I have a rolodex of ideas."

"I prefer the direct route." I don't play games. If someone pisses me off, I tell them. We discuss and then we move on. Unless I kill the person, then I bury him before I move on.

Brody barks out a laugh. "I'm glad you're on my side."

"Who said I'm on your side?"

"Your paycheck," he says and hangs up.

I've barely set my phone on my desk when it rings again. I groan. More work I don't have time for. But when I pick up my phone to answer, it isn't work. It's Fender.

I hit deny. Let him stew for a while. He deserves it. How dare he talk to my employer about my workload? Who does he think he is? He's my boyfriend, not my keeper. Leia Wilson can take care of herself.

I get back to work and my spreadsheets. I don't know how much time has passed when someone knocks on the door.

I sigh before standing and stretching my back. I'm entering the living room when the door bursts open and Indigo rushes inside.

"Whoa. What's the rush? Is Isla okay?" Shit. I've been ignoring my phone. I'm a crap mom.

Indigo stops me before I can run out the door. "Isla's fine."

My brow wrinkles. "Why did you burst in here if my daughter's fine?"

"Something's happened."

My heart jumps in my chest. "Is Fender okay? Is the band okay?"

Shit. I collapse on the sofa. I've been ignoring his calls because I'm pissed with him. What if those calls were my last chance to speak to him? I bury my face in my hands. I'm a horrible, spiteful person.

Indigo wraps an arm around my shoulders. "Fender's fine. Everyone in the band is fine. They're on their way home now."

"On their way home? They aren't supposed to get back until tomorrow night."

"They're coming home early because of what happened."

"I swear to all things holy if you don't stop being mysterious, I'm going to give Cash a dog to terrify Katy Purry."

She gasps. "My cat hates dogs."

"Start talking or I'm getting Cash the biggest dog I can find. What kind of dog is bigger than a Great Dane?"

"The press found out about you."

"About me? Why would the press care about me?"

"Because you're dating Fender who's a member of one of the most popular bands in the world."

My nose wrinkles. "Are the fans going to send me hate mail? I can close my social media accounts. Social media sucks anyway. In fact, this might be a good lesson for Isla about social media."

"Will you stop dissing social media and listen to me?"

I motion for her to proceed.

"The press know you live in Winter Falls."

"They know where I live?"

"Not exactly where you live but they know you're in Winter Falls."

I jump to my feet and rush to the door. "We need to get to Isla."

"She's safe at the community center. Cedar won't let them inside."

I glare at her. "Would you entrust the safety of your child to anyone else?"

Her eyes light with understanding. "Let's go."

I sprint to the community center with Indigo on my heels. I burst through the doors and rush inside.

"Isla!"

She peeks out of a room. "Geez, Mom. Why don't you yell my name louder? I don't think they heard you in Japan."

"Isla."

She opens her mouth – probably to whine some more – when she catches the look on my face. "What is it? What happened? Is Fender okay?"

"Fender's fine, but I need you to come with me." I hold out my hand.

"Is it Grandma and Grandpa?"

I frown. I have no idea if anyone would even notify me if my parents were injured or dead. They cut me out of their lives completely. I doubt I'm mentioned in their will. I don't want any money from them anyway.

"Listen." I kneel in front of Isla while Indigo stands next to us gasping for breath.

"Sorry." She bends over and clutches her stomach. "Not a runner."

"You know how Fender's famous?" I begin.

"Duh. He's in a band."

"Sometimes famous people have trouble with the press."

"Press?" Indigo snorts, and I glare at her. "Sorry. I'll be quiet now."

"What kind of trouble?" Isla asks.

"Well," I stall. How do I explain the paparazzi to an eleven-year-old whose never been in the limelight before? "Who's your favorite singer?"

"Taylor Swift."

"Do you read what she's doing? Where she's going? What she eats? What she's wearing?"

"Yeah."

"It's the same with Fender. His fans want to know what he's up to."

"Okay."

She obviously doesn't understand what I'm saying. I'm un-prepared since I did not have 'explain paparazzi to my daughter' on my bingo card today.

"His fans adore him and they want to know if he has a girlfriend."

"You're his girlfriend."

"I am."

Her eyes widen when understanding hits her. "They want to know all about us."

I nod. "They do. And it's possible they're coming to Winter Falls."

Indigo waves her phone at me and mouths *they're here.*

My heart beats against my chest. They're here. Will they harm my child? Screw that. No one is getting their hands on Isla.

"Cedar!" I shout.

The manager of the community center lumbers out of a door. "What do you need, Leia?"

I don't hesitate. "A weapon."

"Shovel work for you?"

I grin. "A shovel is excellent."

Indigo shackles my wrist and drags me to a quiet corner. "You can't go after the paps with a shovel."

"Why not?"

"They have cameras."

Excellent. "Those cameras are fragile and worth a lot of money."

She squeezes my hand. "Promise me not to break any of their cameras."

I shrug. "No promises."

Cedar returns with a shovel and hands it to me. "I'll keep Isla safe here."

Isla's eyes are about the size of saucers. "What are you doing, Mom?"

"Don't worry." I wink. "I got this."

I squeeze her shoulder before lifting the shovel and marching out of the community center. I scan Main Street and notice several reporters standing on the steps of the courthouse. The police are barring them from entering. I head their way.

"Who's Fender's girlfriend?" a reporter shouts at the chief of police.

He crosses his arms over his chest. "No comment."

"What's her name?"

"No comment."

"Where does she live?"

"No comment."

The chief notices me and shakes his head. Does he seriously think he can warn me away from protecting my child?

"Looking for me?" I ask and the group whirls around to face me.

"What's your name?"

"Where do you live?"

"Are you engaged to Fender?"

"Are you pregnant?"

"Are you living together?"

I ignore their questions to ask one of my own. "No one asked me if I was on the high school softball team."

I swing the shovel like a bat. "State champion three years in a row."

"You can't hit us with a shovel!"

"It's manslaughter!"

"The police will arrest you!"

"I will?" the chief asks. "You're trespassing in my town."

"Our town," Brody corrects him from behind me.

I glance over my shoulder at him to discover he's not alone. He brought his brothers with him. All of whom are scowling at the paparazzi.

"And mine," Sage says. She's standing with the gossip gals who are giving the reporters their best 'I'm disappointed in you'-looks.

"And mine," Rowan adds as he comes to stand next to me.

"It's Rowan Hansley."

"He won the Super Bowl a few years ago."

"Rowan! Rowan! Over here."

"Time for you to leave," I shout as they begin throwing questions at Rowan.

The police form a line and start down the stairs forcing the reporters to do the same or get trampled upon. When they reach the street, the natives of Winter Falls herd them in the direction of White Bridge.

"The press are protected by the constitution!"

"We aren't making any laws to prohibit the press," the chief of police says. "But we do have a law prohibiting those gas-guzzling vehicles." He motions to where a line of cars are parked on the street. "The tow truck's on the way."

"You can't tow our vehicles," one of the reporters claims.

The chief smiles. "Watch me."

"Screw this," he mutters before hurrying to his car.

The rest of the paps follow him. They get into their cars and drive away. Only when I can't see any of their vehicles anymore do I blow out a breath.

"That was awesome!" Petal shouts.

"We need to have new t-shirts made," Feather says.

I turn away from them as they begin to discuss what to have printed on their new t-shirts.

I thank Brody and his brothers as well as Rowan before starting toward the community center with Indigo.

"I need to check on Isla," I say.

"I never knew you were a softball champion."

I wink at her. "I wasn't."

Chapter 29

I love you – three little words Fender has never said to anyone before

FENDER

"We're almost there," Dylan says and I realize I'm grinding my teeth. I don't stop, though. I can't. I won't be able to relax until Leia and Isla are in my arms.

Jett points to the police car up ahead. "Uh-oh, it's the fuzz."

"Don't worry." Cash continues to defy the speed limit as he passes the police car. "It's my brother, Peace. He'll escort us to Leia's house."

I'm still shocked every time Cash says 'brother'. When we met, he was an orphan with no family to his name. Now, he has six half-brothers. One of whom is Leia's boss.

Leia. I hope she's okay. The only thing I know is how the paps swarmed the courthouse but were forced away by the town's residents.

What happened to Leia and Isla? Were they there? Did the paps upset them? Did they tell my girls lies about me to get their reactions? Did they believe the lies?

We reach the street where Leia's house is and I grab the door handle. As soon as Cash slows down, I open the door and jump out.

"You could have waited until I stopped," Cash shouts after me.

I ignore him and rush toward the house.

"She's okay," Peace calls from the open window of his police car.

I won't believe she's okay until I see it with my own eyes. I reach the porch and the door flies open.

"Fender!" Isla yells before throwing herself at me.

I catch her. I will always catch her. This precious girl has burrowed herself under my skin and I'm not letting her go.

"Are you okay, cutie pie?"

"I missed you."

I kiss her hair. "I missed you, too."

"Really?"

"Of course, I missed you. I had no one to play tag with the entire week. Who was I supposed to play with? Jett? Everyone knows he cheats."

Isla giggles. "Gibson cheats, too."

Leia clears her throat. I rake my gaze over her. She doesn't have any outer injuries, but she is standing in the doorway with her arms crossed over her chest and her mouth set in a flatline. My firecracker is pissed.

"Isla, baby girl. Go to your room. Fender and I need to talk," Leia orders.

I set Isla on her feet.

"But he just got back," she pouts.

"Fender and I need to discuss adult stuff," Leia says. I hope adult stuff isn't code for her dumping my ass.

Isla's nose wrinkles. "Are you going to kiss and be disgusting?"

I chuckle as I herd her inside the house. "Kissing isn't disgusting."

"Yes, it is. Astro kissed me at school. His lips were cold. It was gross."

I growl. "Who's Astro? Why did he kiss you? Did you want him to kiss you?"

Isla rolls her eyes. "You're as bad as Mom." She skips to her room without answering my questions.

I close the door and shut out Gibson and Jett who are standing in the front yard watching the show. They whine and complain but I ignore them. They're not important now. Leia is.

I step toward her. I want her in my arms. I need to feel for myself that she's uninjured but her nostrils flare as she stares at me, and I freeze.

"You're okay? The paps didn't hurt you?"

She snorts. "The paps didn't hurt me. I didn't give them the chance."

Relief pours through me at her words. The vultures didn't hurt her. "What did you do, firecracker?"

"I showed them my softball skills."

"I didn't know you played softball."

She smirks. "I don't."

"You didn't hurt anyone?"

She rolls her eyes. "Why does everyone keep asking me if I hurt anyone? All I did was brandish a shovel at a bunch of reporters in front of the chief of police."

I hope I'm mishearing her. "You brandished a shovel?"

She shrugs. "Brandish sounds cool. In actuality, I carried it on my shoulder."

Leia is barely five feet tall and reminds me of a pixie with her blonde hair and blue eyes. But if anyone can pull off intimidating a bunch of paps, it's her.

"I wish I had been there." I clear my throat. "I'm sorry I wasn't."

She waves away my apology. "It was bound to happen sometime. My only concern is keeping Isla safe."

"We'll keep Isla safe. After the incident with Virginia, the town is on the lookout for anyone who doesn't belong."

"I figured as much since Indigo got a message to let her know when the press had arrived."

"You seem awful calm about the situation."

"I'm not an idiot. I knew what I was getting myself into when we started this relationship."

I can't handle it any longer. I can't be in the same room as Leia and not touch her. Especially not after being apart for the past week. It's torture. I grasp her hands. Relief pours through me when she doesn't pull away.

"It's one thing to know you can be hounded by the press. It's another thing to experience it."

"Stop walking on eggshells. I'm fine. Isla's fine. The press can go stuff themselves."

I haul her into my arms, but she stops me with a hand to my chest and steps away.

"What's wrong? You said you were fine. Is this a trick? You say you're fine but it really means you're pissed off?"

She scowls at me. "I don't play games. If I say I'm fine, I'm fine."

"You look pissed off."

"Because I am."

I growl. How is this not playing games?

"Not about the paps. You can't stop them from doing what they do. It's part of the package of being with you."

"Okay. If you're not mad at me because of them, what are you mad about?"

"What am I mad about? You really have to ask?"

Is this another trick question? Before I have a chance to figure it out, she continues.

"How dare you? How dare you speak to Brody about my workload? How dare you speak to my boss as if I'm some little woman who can't handle her own life?" She pokes me in the chest. "You don't own me, Fender Hays."

I capture her hand and place it against my heart. "But you own me."

"Don't try to deny it. You…" Her brow wrinkles. "What did you say?"

"I said you own me. Heart and soul."

Her nose wrinkles in confusion. My little firecracker is adorable when she's confused.

"Hold on. Did you just try to end an argument by claiming I what? Own your heart and soul?"

I kiss her nose. "I love you, firecracker."

"No. No. No." She tugs on my hand but I don't allow her to retreat.

"No what? I don't love you?"

"No, you can't end an argument by claiming to love me. It's cheating. I'm supposed to be mad at you."

I smirk. "But you aren't."

Her eyes narrow and she spits daggers from them at me. "Don't gloat."

I clear my throat and wipe the smirk from my face. "I love you, Leia." I raise a hand to stop her when she opens her mouth to speak. "I talked to Brody because I wasn't allowing the woman I love to work herself to an early grave."

"You have to let me fight my own battles, Fender."

"But you weren't fighting this one, firecracker. You were letting Brody stomp all over you."

She growls. "You're lucky I love you, Fender or I'd seriously kick your ass right now. I don't care how you're a foot taller than me. I will—"

She loves me? I slam my lips down on hers. She gasps in surprise and I shove my tongue into her mouth. Her tart taste hits me and I moan. How does she taste better every single time I kiss her?

I pinch her chin and tilt her head so I can deepen the kiss. She moans and her tongue meets mine. I wrap my arms around her and lift her up. She wraps her legs around me and I walk forward until her back hits the wall.

A thump sounds before Isla shouts, "I'm okay."

Leia wrenches her lips from mine. "Did you break anything?"

"No!"

"Good," she mutters before she jolts and her eyes widen. "We're in the living room. We can't do this here." She wiggles to be let down.

"Don't move," I growl at her. "You love me?"

Her eyes cloud in confusion. "I didn't ….Crap. I did say those words, didn't I?"

"Say them again," I order.

"No."

I nip her bottom lip. "Say them again and I'll say them again."

"You can say them anyway."

I don't deny her. I can't deny her anything. She has me wrapped around her little finger.

"I love you, Leia Wilson. I've never said those words to anyone before."

She frowns. "You've never said I love you before? Not even to Vicki?"

"No." I thought I loved Vicki but I never actually said the words. And now I'm glad I didn't. I'm glad Leia is the first woman I can give those words to.

"What about your mom?" I scowl. "Someday you have to tell me about her."

I nod. "I will. I promise."

There's a knock on the door before Jett shouts, "Can Isla come out to play?"

I set Leia on her feet. "I'll deal with the idiot."

"Idiots," Gibson corrects.

I open the door and snarl at Gibson and Jett. "Leave."

"Fender." Leia slaps my shoulder. "Be nice."

"Why?"

She sighs. "I apologize for him. He thinks he's an actual king when in reality he's only the King of the Grumps."

"He's going to be thanking us in less than a minute," Jett claims.

I grunt. Why would I thank these yahoos?

"Assuming mama bear lets Isla come over for a slumber party at our house," Gibson says.

"We have movies, popcorn, candy, and a tent."

Jett barely finishes speaking before Isla shrieks. "Say yes, Mom!"

Leia worries her bottom lip as she studies Gibson and Jett.

"We'll be next door. If anything happens, you can be there in seconds," Jett says.

"Okay," Leia gives in and Isla rushes out of the house.

"Bye, Mom. Bye, Fender. See you in the morning!"

"You owe us," Jett says before following her.

"Big time," Gibson adds.

I shut the door in his face.

"What are we going to do without Isla?" Leia asks with a mischievous smile.

I stalk toward her. She giggles before running away. I chase after her. I will always chase after her.

Chapter 30

Worship – what Fender plans to do to Leia for the rest of his life

FENDER

I catch Leia in the hallway and throw her over my shoulder.

"Help! I'm being kidnapped by grumpystiltskin."

I tap her ass. "Quiet or I'll spank you."

"You wouldn't dare," she snarls but the way she's wiggling on my shoulder lets me know she's intrigued by the idea. I file the information away for future use. Not today. Today is about showing her I love her. Not about pushing her boundaries.

I lay her on the bed before covering her with my body. "I'm going to worship every single inch of you with my mouth."

Her breath catches. "Every single inch?"

I glide my teeth along her neck until I reach her ear and nip the lobe. "Every single inch."

She squirms beneath me. "This sounds as if it may take some time. You better get started."

I push up on my elbows to gaze into her sparkling blue eyes. "Impatient?"

"More like curious." She shrugs and feigns nonchalance. The way she rubs her legs together makes her a liar.

"I love you, Leia, but you are a horrible liar."

"Am not."

I grunt.

"I am not."

I chuckle at her insolence. I usually hate arguments and disagreements, but with Leia, I get off on them. I get off on pretty much everything she does. I'm addicted to her.

I kneel in front of her and grasp the hem of her t-shirt. I snort when I read what it says. *So apparently I have attitude.*

"Did you wear this when you confronted the paps?"

"What's wrong with my t-shirt?" she asks proving the saying is appropriate.

I lift the t-shirt up and over her before throwing it on the floor. Her breasts push up against her white bra. No lacey bra today. I don't give a fuck. Leia could be wearing a ratty robe with her hair up in curlers and she'd still be sexy.

"Can't lick every inch of you while you're wearing this. It's gotta go."

She lifts her arms above her head. It's an invitation I can't refuse. I will never refuse.

I reach around for the opening in the back.

"There's no fastening."

"At all?"

"Nope."

"Challenge accepted."

I consider ripping the garment off of her but I don't want to hurt Leia. Instead, I grasp the bottom of the bra before tugging it up her body and over her head.

Her breasts bounce with the movement. I know where I'm going to start worshipping her.

I lick a circle around her nipple while my hand kneads and massages her other breast. Soon enough she's squirming beneath me. Her hands latch onto my ears and I immediately stop.

"No touching."

"No touching at all?" She pouts.

"Not until I say you can."

"But I want to touch your body."

"And you will." I pause. "Later."

"What if I want to touch you now?"

"Do I need to tie your hands to the headboard?" Her mouth drops open and interest sparks in her eyes. "Do you want me to tie your hands?"

"Maybe."

I lean across her to reach the top drawer of her nightstand where I know she keeps her scarves. I pull out two. "Still with me?"

She responds by reaching her hands above her and latching onto the slats of the headboard. My cock – already hard and ready to get the show on – strains against my zipper.

I quickly tie her wrists, making sure she has some range of movement. I kneel and study her beneath me. Her breasts are jutting out, her nipples hard points aching for my attention, and her legs are crossed as she rubs her thighs together.

She's a dream. My dream. The dream I denied myself for years after what happened with Vicki. I'm done denying myself what I want. This woman is mine.

I pull her legs apart and kneel in between her thighs. "You're the most beautiful woman I've ever seen."

"I'm a sure thing, grumpy dude. No need to flatter me."

"Pay attention, Leia. I plan to flatter you as often as I want. And I want to often."

I don't give her a chance to respond before I meld my lips to hers. She opens up to me and I dive in. While I explore every inch of her mouth, my hands pluck and pinch at her nipples until her legs wrap around me and she rubs her core against my cock.

If she continues this, I'm going to come in my jeans. I refuse to come in my jeans.

I end the kiss to ask, "Do I need to tie your legs up?"

She immediately stops rubbing. "No."

"You sure? There are more scarves."

She contemplates her answer for a moment before saying, "I'm sure."

"Then, behave and lay still."

"How am I supposed to lay still when your hands are on me?"

"You enjoy my hands on you?" She nods and I trail a finger from her wrist up to her shoulder. "This way?" I draw my other hand from her waist to the underside of her breast. "Or this way?" I trace a finger around her areola. "Or how about this?" I ask as I pinch her nipple.

Her head falls back and she moans. "Yes."

"Don't move your legs," I warn before covering her breast with my mouth. I begin to suck and lick her.

She squirms beneath me but she doesn't move her legs.

"Good girl," I mutter against her skin which puckers in response. "I think you deserve a reward."

"I do. I definitely do."

I chuckle as I unsnap her shorts and draw the zipper down. I pull her shorts and her panties down her hips and off her legs.

Leia's laid out in front of me with no clothes except for the scarves around her wrists. My heart pounds in my chest as satisfaction sweeps through my body. This is my woman. The one I love. The one I plan to keep forever.

The one I'm going to plant babies in when she's ready. I hope she's ready soon. Isla needs a little sister who's a carbon copy of Leia.

I draw my hands up her inner legs until I reach her core.

"Spread your legs for me, firecracker."

She opens up wide for me and I fit my shoulders between her legs. I kiss my way up her thighs until I'm nearly at her center when I discover a freckle. I kiss it.

"You have a little freckle. Right here." I kiss it again. "It's mine now."

"You can have it if you quit messing around."

"Messing around? You don't enjoy messing around in bed with me?"

She glares down at me. "You know what I mean."

"I do?"

I trace a finger up and down her outer lips. She moans and her head falls back. "Do you mean this?"

I open her lips and circle her clit with my thumb. "Or this?"

I sink a finger into her. "Or this?"

She moans. "Yes, the last one."

I pump my finger in and out of her a few times. "This way?"

"More."

I remove my finger and her eyes fly open. I lick my finger and her eyes flare.

"I said I was going to worship every inch of you with my mouth. Time to get started."

I rub my nose up and down her core before I latch onto her clit with my mouth and suck. Her back bows off the bed. I place an arm around her waist to keep her where I want her. And then it's time to feast.

I lick and suck at her clit until I figure out which movements make her squirm and which make her breath hitch. Once I have those clues memorized, I go about driving her crazy.

She pulls on her restraints as she thrashes from side to side. I don't want her thrashing. I want her calling my name. Begging me for release.

I pluck and pinch at her nipples while my mouth continues to torture her clit.

"Fender," she groans.

I grunt and her thighs tremble.

"Please," she pleads.

I grunt again.

"Please. Please. Please," she chants.

I spear her with two fingers and her walls immediately convulse around me as she comes. "Yes!"

I lift my head to watch as the pleasure rolls through her. It's a sight I want to see every day for the rest of my life. She's a sight I want to see every day for the rest of my life.

I feel pre-cum gather on my cock. I grit my teeth. My cock will get his chance. But Leia comes first. She will always come first.

I continue to thrust my fingers in and out of her as she rides out her orgasm. When she collapses on the bed, I get to my feet. Her eyes pop open to watch me as I undress.

"Is it my turn to lick every inch of your body?" she asks.

I grunt.

"I want to lick your tattoos."

I'm afraid my cock will go on strike if he doesn't get a chance to bury himself in her soon. "Next time."

I finish undressing and lay on top of her before hitching my cock at her entrance.

She wraps her legs around me and flips me onto my back. I lift my brow at her and she raises her hands – scarves and all – in the air.

"I say this time."

"How?"

She grins. "Isla went through a *Masked Magician* phase."

I should have known my firecracker wouldn't stay where I told her to.

"My turn," she says before her lips meet my chest and she begins to kiss and lick my tattoos while rubbing her core over my cock.

"You have two minutes before I take charge."

Her eyes sparkle in challenge. "You can try."

I bark out a laugh. I've never had this much fun in bed with a naked woman before. I guess this is how it feels to love someone.

I thread my hands through her hair and yank to lift her head. "Love you, firecracker."

Her eyes warm and her face goes soft. "Love you, too, grumpy face."

All the shit with Vicki. All the sorrow. It was worth it to get to this moment. I'm never letting Leia go.

Chapter 31

False alarm – When you're scared about a problem but then discover the problem isn't a problem after all

LEIA

I flip through my agenda in search of the information Brody wants. Where is it?

I give up on flipping through the daily calendar and turn to the month in overview. Maybe it'll give me a clue where I should look next.

I frown when I notice what day it is. That can't be right.

I check my computer. It says the same day.

I check my phone. Also, the same day.

My watch. Again. The same day.

Shit. Shit. Shit. My period is late.

I blow out a breath. This can't be right. I can't be pregnant. I take my pill every day. I never skip a day. I haven't been ill and thrown up my pill. It's not possible I'm pregnant.

But the proof is staring me in the face. I missed my period. And the whole dang reason I take the pill is to have a regular period.

This is a disaster. Fender is going to think I'm trying to trap him.

Take a pregnancy test.

For once my inner voice is the voice of reason. Okay. I'll take a test. It'll prove I'm not pregnant and all will be well.

I stop with my hand on the front door. I can't buy a test in Winter Falls. I haven't lived here long, but I'm pretty certain the whole town would be wagging their tongues about my being pregnant before I managed to take the test and figure out if I was even pregnant!

But I can't go to White Bridge either. I don't have a car. The town has cars the residents can use but those are for emergencies. This is an emergency but I can't exactly tell anyone what the emergency is.

Why did I think living in a small town would be fun? I must have been delusional.

Think, Leia. Think. Where can I get a car?

I'm not borrowing Fender's. My phone rings. Speak of the devil. I ignore the call. I'll deal with him later.

Who else owns a vehicle in Winter Falls? Most people don't since there's no need for a car if you live and work in town.

Virginia walks to the library for work. And Indigo walks to the school.

Wait a minute. Indigo walks to school, but Cash has a car. What are the chances I can borrow it?

"Can I ask for a favor? No questions asked?" I ask the second she picks up the phone.

She giggles. "Can I ask what the favor is?"

"I need a car to go to White Bridge."

"I'm going with you. I won't ask questions now. But you will tell me what's happening before the end of the day," she demands.

"You drive a hard bargain."

"I can't protect you from the busybodies of town if I don't know what's happening."

I hate how she's right. I blow out a breath. "Okay. How soon can you be here?"

"On my way."

When Indigo arrives in Cash's flashy car, I nearly change my mind. How the hell are we going to keep this mission secret in that thing?

But I don't have a choice. I need to know. Am I pregnant?

I get into the car and Virginia waves from the backseat. "Sorry. Indigo insisted."

"You need all your besties with you for a secret mission," Indigo says as she drives out of town.

I snort. "A secret mission? In this car?"

"If anyone asks, we're getting manicures in White Bridge," Indigo says instead of answering me.

I lift my hands. "What happens when we come back without pretty nails?"

"Oh, we're getting manicures. I already made the appointment."

"How do you know we have time? Maybe my 'mission' requires lots of time."

Indigo glances over at me and winks. "Pretty sure it doesn't."

Virginia changes the conversation to books, and I breathe a sigh of relief. While they discuss books, I contemplate what I'm going to do. I'm not ready for another baby. I'm barely holding it together as it is. Being a single mom of two kids was not on my bingo card for this year.

You wouldn't be a single mom.

I roll my eyes at my inner voice. How does she know Fender isn't going to run as fast as he can away from me when he discovers I'm pregnant?

No. I'm not pregnant. It's some kind of fluke.

Indigo pulls into a strip mall and parks in front of a drugstore.

"Do you want us to come in with you?"

Virginia groans. "Dylan will have a nursery built before we return if I'm seen buying a pregnancy test."

There's my confirmation. They know what's happening.

"You can stay in the car."

Indigo snatches my hand before I can get out. "No way. You're not doing this alone."

Relief courses through me at her words. I did all of it – the pregnancy test, the doctor visits, the birth – alone the first time. I don't want to go through it alone again.

"We got you, bestie," Indigo whispers before dropping my hand and opening the door.

When Virginia crawls out of the backseat, I try to stop her. "No. I don't want you in trouble with Dylan."

"I'm not letting you do this alone either."

Tears well in my eyes. "You guys are the best."

Indigo rolls her eyes. "Duh. I've been telling you how awesome I am for months now."

I inhale a deep breath and straighten my spine before marching into the drugstore. I don't bother pretending to browse. I march straight to the pregnancy tests.

"Which one should you buy?" Virginia asks.

I grab three different ones. "It's always good to be certain."

"Do you have a restroom?" Indigo asks as I check out.

The clerk glances down at my purchases and sighs. She points to the back. "Try not to spend all day in there."

"I don't think we're the first women to do this," Virginia mutters as we enter the restroom together.

There's one toilet, no stall, and zero privacy.

"Maybe you two can wait in the hallway."

Indigo rolls her eyes. "You don't have anything we don't have."

Virginia grasps Indigo and whirls her around. "We won't look."

"I wasn't going to look," Indigo claims.

"Seriously? You were staring at Leia like she's a science experiment."

"It is science."

I tune out their bickering while I open the three packages and lay them side by side on the sink next to the toilet. The instructions claim the tests will work even if it's not morning. I hope they're right.

"You can turn around now," I tell Indigo and Virginia once I've peed on the sticks.

"I've set my alarm to three minutes." Indigo waves her phone in the air.

"What are you going to do if you're pregnant?" Virginia asks.

Pregnant! No. This is to prove I'm *not* pregnant. But what if I am? I clasp my chest as my breathing becomes labored. Did someone steal all of the air in here?

Indigo slaps Virginia's shoulder. "Way to go. You're giving the pregnant lady a heart attack."

Pregnant lady? My knees weaken and I sway to the side. Indigo wraps an arm around my waist before I faceplant on the floor.

"Why don't you sit down?"

I scan the utilitarian restroom. "Where?"

"On it." Virginia places toilet paper on the toilet seat until it's covered. "This is as good as it gets."

Indigo helps me sit and I drop my face into my palms. "This is a disaster."

"It's not a disaster. You have a good job. A good home. A supportive family. And a man who loves you. You're going to be fine."

I whip my head up. "Family? My parents haven't deigned to talk to me since they found out I was pregnant at seventeen and my grandparents died when Isla was a baby."

"Not those jerks. I mean us." She motions between Virginia and herself. "We're your family."

"And you have Isla and Fender, too," Virginia points out.

"But how long will I have Fender if I'm pregnant. You don't know what happened to him. He's going to lose his mind."

I only realized I love Fender a little while ago. I'm not ready to lose him. I've been making plans to keep him forever. I groan and drop my head into my hands again.

"What do—" Indigo is cut off when her alarm beeps. "It's time."

I swallow the lump in my throat. It's time. I don't want to look. Maybe if I don't look I can pretend this isn't happening. I can be one of those women who show up at the hospital in labor who didn't realize they were pregnant.

"Panic's over. You're not pregnant," Indigo declares.

I gasp. "You looked."

She waves the instructions in the air. "It says you have to check at three minutes. Otherwise, you can get a false positive."

Virginia squeezes my shoulder. "You okay?"

Of course, I'm okay. This is the outcome I wanted. I don't want to be pregnant. Except a tiny piece of me is disappointed. It was already imagining a little boy with Fender's green eyes running around playing with Princess.

I shove those thoughts away. I'll think about them later. Much later. In a few years perhaps.

I force myself to my feet. "Why did I miss my period if I'm not pregnant?"

"It says here a missed period can be the result of stress." Indigo points to an article on her phone. "You have been under a lot of stress lately."

I wrinkle my nose. "No, I haven't."

Virginia raises her eyebrows. "No? You didn't move to a new town with your daughter? You didn't get a new job? You didn't fall in love?"

"Fine. Fine. Fine. There may be some stress. But I'm used to stress."

"Let's chalk it up to stress." Indigo winds her arm through mine. "Now, who's ready to get some pretty nails."

"Only if they have liquor at this nail salon."

"It can be arranged." She winks. I allow her to drag me out of the store and into the car.

Disappointment sits heavy in my stomach. I rub my middle. Go away. I'm not disappointed. I don't want Fender's baby.

Liar.

Chapter 32

Dumbass – A person who hasn't dealt with his past and therefore screws up his future

FENDER

I frown when Dylan and Cash walk into the house I share with Gibson and Jett.

"What are you guys doing here?" Gibson asks.

Cash slaps his feet off the couch and sits. "We can't visit our bandmates without an appointment?"

Jett rolls his eyes. "You don't have time for us since you're in love. Blech."

Dylan points to me. "He's in love, too, and you aren't bothering him."

Jett glares at me. "Because he hides his food when we do."

"Not just the food," Gibson mutters.

Dylan meets my gaze and I nod. Yes, I'm hiding Gibson's beer. No, it's not helping. He's drinking entirely too much.

Drinking on tour every night I can understand. The excitement and adrenaline make it hard not to. But at home? When we're on break? We need to confront Gibson soon. Before he's completely out of control.

"Indy and Virginia went to White Bridge with Leia to treat themselves to manicures," Cash says.

What? Leia didn't tell me. She told me she needed to work this morning. I offered to look after Isla but she has some scout outing.

"When was this decided?" I ask.

Dylan shrugs. "This morning. It was a last minute thing."

"They should be home soon," Cash begins. "In the meantime, I thought we could discuss which song to release as our next single."

Dylan scratches his chin. "Do we need to bring out a new single? *Resurrect* is still at the top of the charts."

"We don't have to release the new single right away. But we should figure out which song is next."

"We should let the fans decide," Gibson says.

"How?" Cash asks.

While the band discusses which song to release as our next single, I stare out the window at the house next door. How did Leia leave without me realizing it? Did she sneak out? Is she hiding something from me?

I shake those thoughts out of my mind. Leia isn't Vicki. She's the woman I love. Vicki was a bump in the road.

I spot a car traveling down the street. It stops in front of Leia's house, and Leia jumps out while waving to the occupants.

"Going," I grunt. I don't wait for a reply before heading next door to Leia's house.

"Did I forget something?" Leia asks when she opens the door to my knock. She smiles. "Oh, it's you."

She pushes up on her tiptoes to kiss me. I keep the kiss short. I have questions.

"Did you finish your work?"

She blows out a breath. "Not yet."

I nod to the bag in her hand. "Did you go shopping?"

Panic lights her eyes. "N-n-no."

"You didn't go shopping? What's in the bag?"

She rolls her eyes but the panic is still clear to see. "It's a drugstore bag. Necessities."

I cross my arms over my chest and glare at her. "If your bag is full of necessities, why are you panicking?"

"I'm not panicking," she says as she retreats down the hallway.

I stalk after her. "Why are you lying to me?"

"I'm not lying." She stuffs the bag in the kitchen garbage.

"I thought the bag was full of necessities. Why are you throwing it away?"

"Can you give me a moment?"

"A moment? A moment to what? Come up with a lie for what you were doing today?"

She rears back. "You make it sound as if I was cheating on you."

I raise an eyebrow. "You weren't?"

She scowls. "I was with Indigo and Virginia."

"Nevertheless. You're hiding something from me." I nod toward the garbage can.

"I need a minute." She stomps down the hallway and the bathroom door slams moments later.

I don't hesitate. I open the garbage can and dig the bag out. I dump the contents on the kitchen counter. Hell. She's pregnant? Wait a minute. No, she isn't. These are all negative.

Is she trying to get pregnant? Is she trying to trap me? Fuck me.

"What are you doing?"

I whirl around at her question and point to the pregnancy tests on the kitchen counter. "What are *you* doing?"

She throws up her arms. "I was late, okay? I didn't know what to do. I panicked and rang Indigo who hurried me off to White Bridge to take these tests. I should have thrown them away at the drugstore."

I growl. "And then you would have never had to tell me."

She shakes her finger at me. "Don't you dare growl at me, Mr. Grumpy Pants."

Usually, I find her little pet names for me adorable. I'm not finding anything adorable today.

"Were you going to tell me any of this?"

"Um, grumpy dude, I just did."

"After I confronted you and forced it out of you."

"I just got home."

"And you didn't tell me you were going to White Bridge either."

"I told you. I panicked."

"You're just like Vicki."

She gasps. "I am not Vicki. I'm not pregnant, asshole."

I motion to the counter. "But you're trying to get pregnant. You want to trap me. Are you even on the pill?"

Her jaw drops open as she stares at me in surprise. What? She thought I wouldn't figure it out. I'm just a dumb bass player in a band. I'm too stupid to realize when a woman is using me.

"I don't recognize you right now."

"Didn't stop you from trying to trap me, though, did it?"

"Trap you? Trap you?" she screeches.

"You get pregnant. I marry you. You don't ever have to worry about money again. No more single mom. No more working. You'd have the easy life."

"You really think those things of me?"

I motion to the counter again. "I have all the proof I need."

Her bottom lip trembles and a lone tear travels down her cheek. I fist my hands before I reach for her. This is a show. She isn't sad. She's pretending.

She inhales a deep breath and her nostrils flare. "Get out."

"Gladly."

"And don't you ever come near me or my kid again, you fucking asshole."

"I'm the asshole? I'm not the one who's trying to trap an innocent man."

"I can't believe I ever thought I loved you. All men are the same. You're just like Charles. Saying pretty words until you get me in bed. And once you have your fill of me, your true self comes out."

I grit my teeth. "Don't blame this on me. I'm not the asshole here."

"No, you're not the asshole. You're the biggest asshole in the entire world."

I growl. "Not the asshole."

"You discovered a bunch of negative pregnancy tests and decided I'm trying to trap you. Total asshole move."

"You didn't tell me about the pregnancy tests."

She throws her arms in the air. "Because I didn't have time! I asked you to give me a minute and instead of giving me time, you dug through my trash like a stalker."

"You were being cagey."

"I was being freaked out because I'm a single mom and I'm not ready to raise two children on my own, dumb ass."

I snort. "You wouldn't raise the children alone once you trapped me into marrying you."

Her face turns red and she points to the door. "Get out!"

"Gladly," I grumble as I march to the door.

The door flies open before I reach it.

"I'm home!" Isla shouts as she skips inside.

I try to soften my face. "Hey, cutie pie."

"You're here!" She throws herself at my legs and I pat her hair as she hugs them. "What are we doing today?"

"I'm sorry, Isla, but Fender's busy today," Leia says before I can figure out how to answer.

Isla juts out her bottom lip. "But I want to play with Fender."

Leia wraps an arm around her daughter and hauls her to her side. "Fender's a busy guy. He's in a big rock band."

She practically sneers the words. As if being in a rock band is bad. At least I'm not living paycheck to paycheck.

"How about the two of us do something fun? I bought some new nail polish today. We can give ourselves pedicures."

"Can I use whatever color I want?" Isla asks.

"Yep. Go to my bedroom and pick out your color while I say goodbye to Fender."

"Bye, Fender!" Isla waves before rushing down the hallway.

The second her daughter is out of view, the smile drops from Leia's face.

"In case this isn't clear, I don't want you anywhere near my daughter."

"Don't be a bitch."

A muscle ticks in her jaw as she reigns in her anger. "I will not allow my daughter to spend time with a man who thinks her mom is trying to use him."

"Fine," I grit out.

She herds me to the door.

"Good riddance, Fender Hays," she mutters as she shuts the door behind me.

Chapter 33

Family – not necessarily the people related to you by blood

LEIA

My heart clenches. I can't breathe. The man I fell in love with thinks I'm trying to trap him into marriage. First Charles and now Fender. I sure do know how to pick 'em.

My eyes itch and tears threaten. But I can't fall apart. Not in front of Isla. She doesn't deserve to be a witness to her mom's drama.

I suck up my tears and promise myself I can fall apart with a bottle of wine later.

I hurry to throw away the pregnancy tests Fender left on the kitchen counter. Once I've disinfected the area – I peed on those sticks – I go to find Isla.

"Did you pick a color?"

She holds up several bottles. "I want to do a different color for each toe."

"Sounds fun."

There's a knock on the door and a smile breaks out on her face. "Maybe it's Fender. Maybe he changed his mind."

Damn Fender for making my daughter fall in love with him.

I force a smile on my face. "Let's go find out."

It's not Fender at the door. Thank goodness because there's only some much pretending I can do.

"Hi, Feather," I greet the gossip gal.

"I was wondering if I can borrow Isla," she says in response.

"Borrow me?" my daughter asks.

Feather puts on a sigh. "I have a problem and I think you're the only person who can help me."

Isla taps her chest. "Me?"

"I've been experimenting with various ice cream flavors, but I can't pick which ones to put in my store."

Isla's eyes widen. "And you want me to help?"

"It would mean eating a lot of ice cream. Are you up to it?"

"I am!" Isla pulls on my shirt. "Can I go, Mom? Can I?"

I nod and she screams.

"Go get a bag," Feather says. "This may take all night."

Isla runs toward her room and Feather captures my hands. "I'm sorry."

"Sorry about what?"

She nods toward the house next door. "We thought he was a good pick."

I don't bother asking how she already knows about the breakup. I wasn't exactly quiet when I kicked Fender out of the house after all. And this town considers eavesdropping a skill to hone.

"You thought wrong. He's a…"

I trail off when I hear Isla return. "Ready!"

"Have fun," I say after I quickly check her bag to make sure she packed more than books and stuffed animals.

They walk off hand in hand with Isla talking a mile a minute about what her favorite ice cream flavors are. I wait until I can't see them anymore before I let out a breath and allow the smile to fall from my face.

I'm shutting the front door when Virginia and Indigo rush up my sidewalk.

"Sorry, we're late," Indigo says. "But we needed supplies."

"Did Feather pick up Isla already?" Virginia asks.

"What's going on?"

Indigo bustles me inside the house and Virginia closes the door behind us.

"Cash called. Fender's destroying the rental house."

"Asshole," I mutter.

Virginia grimaces. "He didn't react well to the pregnancy scare?"

I snort. "Not well? That's putting it mildly. He lost his freaking mind and claimed I'm trying to trap him."

Her brow wrinkles. "How are you trying to trap him? You're not pregnant."

"But I didn't tell him the second I found out I was late, which is proof I'm trying to get pregnant and trap him into marrying me so I can live the life of leisure."

"Um…There might be a reason he flew off the handle," Indigo hedges.

"Yeah. Yeah. I know all about the Vicki situation."

"Vicki situation?" Virginia looks back and forth between me and Indigo. "Who's she?"

I'd love to tell her every single part of the story, but – despite what Fender thinks – I do keep my promises.

"Suffice it to say, she screwed with Fender's head," Indigo says.

"Yep. And he accused me of being her."

She gasps. "What?"

"Yep. I'm a conniving little bitch apparently."

"If you were conniving, you would have made sure he never saw those tests," Virginia points out.

"Great. I'm a conniving little bitch who sucks at being conniving."

"We should prank him," she says and my mouth drops open. "What? I can prank someone."

"Except she's never actually pranked anyone," Indigo whisper-shouts.

"What ideas do you have?" I ask Virginia because the only idea I have right now is to sneak into his room while he's sleeping and turn him into a eunuch. But I can't go to jail. I've got a kid to raise. And there's a possibility causing bodily harm to an ex-boyfriend doesn't send the best message to her.

"We have to hit him where it hurts," Indigo says.

"What does he love?" Virginia asks.

Not me. I thought he did. He convinced me he not only loved me but my daughter as well. I'm such a fool. I should have never let a man near Isla. How am I going to explain to her she's not allowed to spend time with Fender anymore?

Virginia wraps an arm around my shoulders. "I'm sorry, Leia. It was a stupid question."

I wipe the tears spilling from my eyes away. "No, no. You're right. A prank should be against something he loves."

"He's obsessed with food," Indigo offers. "We could raid his refrigerator."

"There's no way we're going to be able to sneak into the house. The entire band is over there now." Virginia points to next door. Since there are no curtains, it's easy to peer into the living room where the entire band can be seen.

"We could lure them away," Indigo suggests.

"And how are we going to lure them away?"

She shrugs. "We can set off fireworks in the front yard and sneak into the back door when they go outside to investigate."

"Where are we going to get fireworks at this time of year. Autumn is around the corner," I remind her.

"We can build our own," Virginia suggests. "There must be a book in the library about how to create explosives."

My eyes widen. "The library has books about explosives?"

Her shoulders deflate. "Maybe not."

"I guess we move onto Plan B." Indigo holds up the bags she's carrying. "Drink wine, eat tons of junk food, and watch trashy movies."

She sets her bags on the coffee table in the living room and starts to empty them. She pulls out chocolate, potato chips, bags of candy, several bottles of wine, a few cans of beer, and three pizzas.

"While trashing Fender," I add.

"I have a great vocabulary." Virginia smirks. "I bet I can think up at least fifty words for jerk."

"Don't forget liar, untrustworthy, sneaky, rat bastard, contemptible, idiot, fool, jackass." I pause to inhale a breath.

Indigo hands me a glass of wine. "Here. This'll help."

I gulp the wine down before collapsing on the sofa. "What am I going to do?"

"You're going to get over the idiot and be all the stronger for it," she says.

"While living next door to him?" I huff. "How am I going to get over him when I see him every day."

"He won't be here all the time. The band starts their tour soon," Virginia says.

"Isla was barely manageable the week Fender was gone for the press release. She's going to be inconsolable now he's gone for good."

I hold out my glass for more wine. Indigo fills it up and Virginia hands me a cracker topped with cheese.

"Hangovers suck," she says.

"I can't believe I thought Fender was different. But he's exactly the same as Charles. Men are unreliable." I wave my wine glass at Indigo and Virginia, and the wine splashes over the edge onto my t-shirt. I ignore it. Who cares about a t-shirt now? "Except your men. They're the exception that proves the rule."

Virginia snatches my glass from me. "Maybe we should get you a sippy cup."

"A sippy cup? Why would I have a sippy cup in my house? I don't have a toddler anymore. Isla's nearly a teenager and I'm never going to have children again."

My bottom lip trembles. "I'm never going to have another child."

Virginia rubs my back. "I thought you were relieved you aren't pregnant."

"A son with Fender's green eyes," I whine before the tears burst from my eyes and I stop all pretense of trying to keep it together.

"He broke my heart. He broke my daughter's heart. I mean, not yet." I use the bottom of my t-shirt to wipe my nose. "She doesn't know yet but her little innocent heart is going to break. Crack! In two. Never to recover. Never to trust a man again."

"Maybe wine wasn't the best idea," Indigo mutters before shoving a piece of sausage at me. "Eat this. It'll make you feel better."

I stare at the piece of meat. "This will make me feel better?"

"I'm not good at consoling people. If you met my mom, you'd understand."

I inhale a deep breath and force myself to get it together. I can't lose it. I have a daughter to care for. I need to be an adult here.

"My mom's horrible, too."

Indigo rubs her hands together. "You think so? Let's compare notes."

Virginia raises her hand. "Excuse me. But I'm pretty sure I win in the horrible mother lottery."

"My mom forced Cash to break up with me and we lost each other for eleven years," Indigo blurts out.

"My mom disowned me when I got pregnant and I haven't heard from her since. She's never met Isla."

Indigo throws her hands in the air. "Fine. You win."

"You forgot about me." Virginia clears her throat. "My mom didn't believe it when my step-brothers tortured me."

I glance around at my friends. "We have some shitty moms, but we've got each other now. No matter what, we have each other."

They wrap their arms around me. Their love and friendship fills me up and soothes over the rough edges of my heartbreak. I'm still devastated but with these two women by my side, I can power through anything.

Chapter 34

Fool – Worse than an idiot

FENDER

I slam the door behind me and the window in the living room rattles. I pick up the first thing I can find – a set of keys – and throw them across the room.

Jett ducks out of the way. "What the fuck, Fender?"

"What's wrong, grumpapottamus?"

At Gibson's question, I start for him. He squeaks and ducks behind the couch to hide.

Jett stands in my way. "What's wrong with you?"

What's wrong with me? I could tell him what's wrong but I'm too pissed to speak. I grunt and grab the TV remote. I throw it across the room and it hits the refrigerator before falling to the floor where it smashes into pieces.

Jett gathers the remote controls for the PlayStation and hugs them to his chest. "Maybe you should go outside and let off some steam."

Gibson peers over the couch at me. "And where there's no one to injure with your wrath."

They think they've seen my wrath? They haven't seen shit yet.

I scan the room for something else I can throw. There isn't much here. This isn't a home. Not the way Leia's house is. *Leia*. How dare she try to use me?

I pick up one end of the coffee table and flip it over. The glasses on the table shatter on the floor. The sound is satisfying. What next?

The door bangs against the wall behind me but I ignore it. I march to the kitchen and whip open a cabinet. It's filled with pots and pans. Not interesting. I move to the next one.

I'm reaching for the glasses when arms wrap around my middle and try to drag me away. I plant my feet. I'm not going anywhere.

"Get away from the kitchen," Cash orders.

"I can't hold him," Dylan mutters as he strains against me.

Cash steps in front of me and together with Dylan they herd me out of the kitchen to the living room where they push me onto the sofa.

"What the hell is going on?" Gibson asks.

"Someone's a fucking idiot," Cash says.

Jett snorts. "Tell us something we don't know."

I surge from the couch but Dylan sits on me to stop me from attacking Jett.

"I'm going to kill him."

"No one's killing anyone," Dylan says.

Gibson raises his hand. "Can someone explain for the kids in the back of the class?"

Cash points to me and I growl at him. "I'm assuming Fender found out Leia took a pregnancy test and promptly lost his mind."

"Leia's pregnant?" Gibson grins. "Congrats, big man."

"Not pregnant," I growl.

"She took a bunch of tests because she was late but she's not pregnant," Cash explains.

"Poor Leia. How is she?" Jett asks.

I grunt. "She's a liar."

Jett's brow wrinkles. "Liar? What did she lie about?"

My nostrils flare. "She's just like Vicki."

Gibson gasps. "Did she say she was pregnant when she wasn't?"

"No."

Jett glares at me. "Did you accuse Leia of being Vicki?"

"She is just like Vicki."

He stomps toward me. "I'm going to kick your ass."

Gibson is right behind him. "I'm in."

I look to Dylan. He's usually the one who calms everyone down, but he doesn't move. "You made your bed. Time to lie in it."

"Fender," Cash begins. "Leia is nothing like Vicki. Why would you accuse her of being Vicki?"

"Because she is. She's trying to trap me."

Jett fists his hands. "Seriously. Let me kick his ass."

I snort. "You can try."

He motions to Gibson standing behind him, Cash next to him, and Dylan beside me. "It's four against one. The odds are in my favor."

I scan the faces of my bandmates, my friends, my family. They're all looking at me with disappointment. What the fuck? They're supposed to be on my side.

Gibson points at me. "He's confused. How can he be confused?"

Dylan sighs. "You hurt one of us. Of course, we're on her side."

"Leia isn't one of us."

Cash growls. "Leia is Indigo's best friend. Don't you dare say she isn't one of us."

"And Isla is my favorite eleven-year-old," Jett adds. "That girl is the shit."

"Too bad her mother is a bitch," I mutter.

Dylan has me in a headlock before I realize what's happening. "Leia is Virginia's friend, too, dipshit. You don't talk about Ginny's friends this way."

I dig my fingers into his arms until he yelps and pulls away. "It's true."

"Did you actually call Leia a bitch to her face?" Cash asks. "What kind of dumbass are you?"

"The kind who fell in love with a woman who doesn't exist."

"Can I smack him?" Jett asks. "Smack some sense right into him?"

Cash pretends to study me. "Not sure you can smack sense into his dumb head right now."

I explode from the sofa. "Why are you on *her* side? She's the one who's trying to trap me into marrying her. She's the one who made me fall in love with a vision of a woman who doesn't exist. She's the one who has the daughter I want for my own. I'm not at fault here."

"Oh boy. Where do we start?" Dylan asks.

"I know where to start." Cash approaches me until he's up in my face. He's several inches shorter than me so I have to glance down at him.

"Why the hell did you assume she's trying to trap you?"

"She didn't tell me she thought she was pregnant."

"And?"

"And she lied."

"She lied? Did she tell you she was pregnant?"

"No."

"Did she tell you she's on birth control and she's not?"

I scowl. "No." I've seen her take her pill in the morning.

"Did she say she wants to marry you?"

"No."

"Dude." Cash sighs. "You made it all about you."

"Does she know about your mom?" Dylan asks.

I glance away.

"That's a no." He sighs. "What about Vicki? Does she know about her?"

I nod.

"She was probably worried and wanted to make sure she wasn't pregnant before she told you about the scare," he says.

"But she didn't tell me. I found the pregnancy tests."

"Where?" Cash asks. "Where did you find them?"

"In her trash."

Dylan widens his eyes. "You dug threw her trash?"

"She was being cagey. Said she needed a moment."

"She said she needed a moment and instead of giving her a moment, you dug threw her trash?" Dylan shakes his head. "Do you even have a clue how a possible pregnancy would scare a single mom who had no support from her family?"

I rub a hand down my face. He's got a point.

Cash points to Leia's house. "And now she's over there crying her eyes out because she's heartbroken."

My heart squeezes in my chest. "Heartbroken?"

"Yeah, dumbass." Gibson rolls his eyes. "Even I can tell how much Leia loves you."

I rub my chest. "Loves me?"

"Yeah, it's confusing to think someone as sweet as Leia would love your grumpy ass."

I snarl at him and he chuckles.

"Now." Cash rubs his hands together. "How are you going to get her back?"

"Get her back?"

"Duh. You love her. She loves you. You fucked up."

Is he right? Did I overreact? I think back to my conversation with Leia. Not once did she bat her eyelashes at me and claim it was all a mistake. No, not my firecracker. She told me exactly how it was before she kicked me out.

Fuck. I screwed up and let the woman I love slip from my fingers. I saw those pregnancy tests and my mind flashed back to Vicki and my mom and I lost it. My mouth started spouting a bunch of bullshit.

I'm worse than an idiot. I'm a fool.

"What do I do?"

Cash smiles. "Easy. You make it up to her."

"You should listen to him," Dylan says. "He knows all about fucking up with the woman you love."

Cash glares at Dylan. "And you've never fucked up with Virginia?"

"I certainly didn't break up with her because I was a scared little bitch."

"I wasn't scared."

"Do you prefer the word scaredy-cat?" Dylan taunts. "Since you do have a cat now."

"I hate cats."

"Guys!" Gibson claps his hands to get everyone's attention. "Can we focus on Fender's problem now? And why am I being the adult here?"

"I was about to ask the same question," Jett mumbles.

"What if Leia won't take me back?"

Fear races through my body. My hands shake and I feel nauseous. I can't lose Leia. I want to spend the rest of my life with her and Isla. I want to build a family with her.

Dylan squeezes my shoulder. "She will."

"After you apologize and admit what a tool you were," Cash adds.

I can apologize. I start to stand.

Dylan pushes me back down. "You can't rush over there now. You need a plan."

"And Leia needs to calm down."

I can't help the smile from forming on my face. My Leia is a force to be reckoned with. "She's a firecracker."

"Now, let's figure out a plan," Cash says.

I can do this. I can grovel. For Leia, I can do anything. And I think I have the perfect way to prove my love to her.

Chapter 35

Grand gesture – When you go all out to apologize because you were a fool

LEIA

"Mom, I'm home."

At Isla's shout, I check my face in the mirror one more time. Eyes no longer puffy? Check. No redness? Check. No sniffy nose? Check. I guess I'm as ready as I'll ever be to break my daughter's heart.

"Hey, baby girl." I greet her with a hug. "How was your night?"

While she babbles on about Feather and ice cream, I lead her to the living room. We sit on the sofa and I wait for her to finish.

"Sounds like you had fun."

"It was awesome. Can I do it again?"

"Some day, sure." I clear my throat. "Now, I have something to discuss with you."

She rolls her eyes. "Is it about Leaf? I didn't mean to say he's a ninny."

I'm not sure how you accidentally call a boy a ninny but I let it go.

"It's about Fender."

"Fender?" She glances around the living room. "Where is he? He didn't stay over? He always stays over when I'm gone. Did you have a fight?"

"We did." She opens her mouth to speak again but I hold up my hand. "Let me finish." And then I wing it. "Fender and I had a big fight and we broke up. During our fight, he said some things, that concern me, and I don't want you hanging out with him anymore."

She crosses her arms over her chest and huffs. "But you said my relationship with Fender is separate from yours. You said I could be friends with him even if you weren't. You lied!"

"I didn't lie. Circumstances changed."

She jumps to her feet. "You're a liar! A big fat liar!"

She stomps off to her room and slams the door. I bury my face in my hands. I feel horrible. Like my heart is being torn from my body. If I hadn't already decided to never date again, this would have changed my mind. I can't chance my daughter getting hurt again.

I won't allow it.

The dryer beeps to indicate it's done – proving life goes on even if you're heartbroken. I make my way to the washroom off the kitchen. Things will improve, I tell myself. Fender will eventually move away and I won't have to see his dumb face ever again.

The doorbell rings and I sigh. I don't need another Winter Falls invasion today. Isla and I need a day together to mourn what we've lost.

"I'll get it!" Isla shouts.

I peek around the corner as she opens the door.

"Fender! You're here."

"Hi, cutie pie."

"I knew Mom was wrong. I knew you still loved me."

She throws herself at him and he captures her in his arms. Arms I will never feel around me again. I rub my hand against my chest but it doesn't alleviate the ache building there.

"Of course, I love you." Fender kisses her nose and tears well in my eyes. How can this man who was a total and complete asshole to me yesterday be this tender with my daughter? Is it all an act? Will the real Fender Hays please step forward? So I can slap him upside his head.

"But I messed up with your mom."

I nearly gasp at Fender's words. I stuff a fist in my mouth to stop myself from responding. I have to hear this.

"I hurt her."

"Why?" Isla asks. "Don't you love her?"

"I love her more than I've ever loved anything in my life."

I bite down on my fist before I can yell at him. He loves me? Why was he an asshole yesterday if he loves me? Why did he say the things he did?

"Then, you need to apologize. Mom always says being honest and apologizing is the best policy."

"I plan to." He leans close to whisper in her ear. "But I need your help."

"What do you want me to do?" Isla's whisper is loud enough for the neighbors to hear.

"Can you get your mom to go outside in fifteen minutes?" He hands her his watch. "When it beeps, I'm ready and you can bring her out."

"Okay."

"Thanks, cutie pie." He starts to back away. "I know you won't let me down."

"Don't let *me* down," she responds and he chuckles.

She shuts the door and I duck back into the laundry room before she can catch me spying on her.

"Who was at the door?" I holler.

"No one."

I don't push her. I don't want her to figure out I was listening in. I return my attention to the laundry. Good thing I don't need to use any mental capacity to fold clothes because my mind is racing.

Fender knows he messed up? He's going to apologize? I glance at the clock. Fifteen minutes can't pass fast enough.

I've somehow managed to fold all the clothes and start a new load of laundry when Isla appears.

"Can I play outside, Mom?"

"Go ahead," I say since I don't want to sound eager.

"Don't you want to come with me?"

"It's okay. I can see you from the kitchen."

She stomps her foot and I cough to hide my amusement. "But I want to play tag. I can't play tag alone."

"Why didn't you say so in the first place?"

She sighs. "Are you ready?"

I set the laundry basket down and follow her outside. My eyes widen at the sight that greets me. I expected to find Fender on his own ready to explain himself. I did not expect the entire band to be in my backyard with their instruments.

Fender motions to the two chairs arranged in front of the band. "Please have a seat. I'd like to play you a song."

"*We'd* like to play you a song," Jett corrects with a wink at Isla.

Isla and I do as we're told. She bounces in her seat. And I'm not much calmer. I'm filled with anticipation. Why are they playing for us? Is this Fender's apology? How can a song be an apology?

Fender clears his throat and picks up the microphone. He's going to sing? Fender doesn't sing. He doesn't even sing back-up. The paps love to speculate about why he doesn't sing. The latest theory is he had surgery on his throat after a bar fight.

Jett taps out a rhythm on a pair of upturned buckets while Dylan and Gibson strum their guitars. And then, Fender begins to sing.

I know I've let you down,
With every promise I betrayed.
I swear upon the heavens,
I'll break down every wall,
I'll tear apart the skies,

To see the love back in your eyes.
I'll shout it from the rooftops,
I'll sing it to the stars above,
I'm sorry my love.
Let me hold you close,
Let me wipe away your tears,
I'll do whatever it takes,
To calm your fears,
With every breath I take,
With every step I make,
I'll prove my love for you,
Is eternal and true.

This is beautiful. The most beautiful apology I've ever heard. I thought after yesterday I'd lost Fender forever. I didn't think a thousand apologies would be enough for me to forgive him. I was wrong. It was one apology. One apology of him doing a thing he's avoided for a decade.

My eyes itch as tears form. I sniff to stop them from falling.

The song ends and Isla jumps to her feet while clapping as hard as her little hands can. "You were awesome!"

"I wrote this song for your mom."

My eyes widen. He wrote this song? Fender doesn't write songs. He plays the bass and is all grumpy at press conferences.

Fender hands the microphone to Cash before approaching me. "Can we talk?"

"Talk to him, Mom," Isla urges. "He loves you. He's sorry."

Fender holds out his hand and I place my hand in his. He pulls me to my feet and leads me to the back door.

"Watch, Isla," Fender orders his bandmates as he draws me into the house.

"I'm sorry," he blurts out the second the door closes behind us.

I cross my arms over my chest. I'm not going to make this easy for him. "Sorry about what?"

"Sorry, I jumped to conclusions. Sorry, I didn't give you a chance to explain. Sorry, I was a jerk."

"A jerk?"

"An asshole?"

"Getting closer."

"An asshole jerk."

I nod. "Good enough."

He frames my face with his hands. "Do you forgive me?"

"I need an explanation. Why did finding those pregnancy tests flip a switch in your mind?"

He blows out a breath. "I told you about Vicki."

And he compared me to her. I scowl.

"I know you aren't her. I'm sorry I said you were." He kisses my forehead. "You've asked about my mom."

I nod. I have. And he has refused to tell me anything about her.

"She wasn't very different from Vicki. She spent her life screwing around with famous men, hoping one of them would marry her. She never got married. The only thing she ended up with was me. A baby she resented since I didn't bring her the man she wanted."

I wrap my arms around his waist. "I'm sorry."

"I thought I'd dealt with it, accepted it, but those pregnancy tests brought it all back."

I can only imagine. At least my parents pretended to love me until I got pregnant. "I'm sorry I didn't handle telling you better."

He growls. "Don't you dare apologize. I was the asshole. Not you."

"I can't disagree with you there."

"Will you forgive me? I wasn't lying in the song. I love you and I can't live without you. You and Isla."

"Forgive him, Mom," Isla yells through the door.

Fender reaches behind me and opens it. My daughter rushes inside and joins our huddle.

"Leia Wilson, I love you. Please forgive me. Allow me to make a family with you and Isla."

Dang it. He had to include Isla? I was barely hanging onto my anger as it was. Oh, who am I kidding. I forgave him the second he picked up the microphone to serenade me.

"I forgive you." He starts to grin but I hold up my finger. "But you can't just write a song and sing to me every time you make me mad."

"Good because songwriting is harder than I thought."

I burst into laughter and he wraps his arms around me. Isla burrows her way in between us and I hold on. I'm holding onto this ride until it stops. And I don't plan for it to stop until I reach the end of my life.

"I love you, Fender."

Chapter 36

Mercy – a woman forced to crazy lengths to help an uncle she never knew existed

MERCY

Come to the party.

I scowl down at the message. I have zero interest in attending a party with rockstars who think they're gods.

Please.

I snort. He's trying to manipulate me. Good luck with that.

You promised.

Crap on a cracker. I did promise.

I don't know what I was thinking when I agreed to fake date Gibson, the rhythm guitarist for the world famous band *Cash & the Sinners*.

The phone rings and Uncle Mercury yells, "Mercy! Answer the phone!"

Ah, yes. Now I remember. I didn't even know I had an uncle a few months ago and now I'm living with him and going to crazy lengths to help him.

"Hello," I answer the phone.

"Go on ahead to the party, Mercy. I'll be there soon to look after your uncle."

"Who is this?"

"It's Cayenne."

Her name doesn't ring a bell.

"Do I know you?"

She sighs. "You should. Now, get to the party. You don't want to miss it." She hangs up without further ado.

What does she know? Maybe I do want to miss the party.

"You better go to the party before those meddling women invade my house. I won't have my house invaded," Mercury says.

"How do you know there's a party?"

"Just because I'm old doesn't mean I don't know what's going on in my town," he grumbles.

I study him. Does he know about my deal with Gibson? Why hasn't he said he knows? What is he planning?

"Go. You can use my car."

He's going to let me drive his pristine 1971 Dodge Charger?

"What?" he asks. "You don't let me drive it anymore anyway. Someone should have the chance to enjoy it."

"Aren't cars with combustion engines banned in Winter Falls?"

He smirks. "Not my car."

There's a story there, but I won't be learning it from my uncle. The man is a closed book. Or maybe a vault of secrets. Either way, he doesn't tell me anything.

I only know about the combustion engine thing because I got pulled over when I first arrived in town. The police officer didn't believe Mercury was my uncle and insisted on following me to his house.

"Someone named Cayenne is on her way over."

Mercury grunts. "I'll handle her."

I'm afraid to ask. My uncle has been known to put a sheet over him and run around the house pretending to be a ghost to scare little kids away. What he doesn't realize is he's putting on a show they will return to again and again.

Honestly, though, I could use a break from Mr. Crotchety. Plus, there's no way I'm missing the chance to drive his muscle car. I snatch the keys from the hook by the door.

"I won't be long."

"Don't hurry back on account of me."

I roll my eyes. Everything I've done for the past few months is for him. But does he appreciate it?

I shut the door behind me, making sure it doesn't rattle, and smile at the car. I'd love to get my hands under her hood.

I run my fingers along the hood as I make my way to the driver's seat. This baby is a thing of beauty. Way better than the piece of junk I drove into town with.

I turn the key and the engine roars to life. The power of the car rumbles under my ass and I grin. I can handle a stupid rock and roll party if it means I can drive this car for a few minutes.

I back out of the driveway and turn the car toward town. The drive to Gibson's house is over in less than five minutes.

I sigh when I arrive. I'd rather spend the day driving through the backroads of Colorado but alas. A promise is a promise.

I'm here.

When I notice Gibson walking toward the car, I open the door and step out. He whistles.

"Are you whistling at me or the car?"

He winks. "Can't it be for both?"

I roll my eyes. It's not bad enough Gibson's a rockstar, he's also a player. That's two strikes against him.

I slam the car door shut. "Let's do this."

"You can at least pretend to be excited."

He must be joking. "Excited about what?"

"Me. I am a catch, you know."

I stop myself before I roll my eyes again. I have a feeling I'm going to be rolling my eyes a lot until our deal is finished.

Gibson holds out his hand. When I scowl at him, he wiggles his fingers. "Girlfriends hold their boyfriend's hand."

"Fine," I mutter.

When our hands meet, a spark of electricity runs from his hand to mine and then through my body heating me from within and sending tingles straight to my core. I gasp. What the hell? I'm not interested in Gibson. My body must be on the fritz.

Gibson stares down at our joined hands. He appears as confused as I am. After a moment, he shakes his head and leads me to the backyard where the party is in full swing.

"Whoa!" A man skids to a stop in front of us. "Who's this? And why are you holding her hand?"

Gibson pushes him. "Why do you think I'm holding her hand?"

"You're afraid she'll run away."

I giggle. He's not wrong.

"Hi!" The man greets me with a smile. "I'm Jett. Dump him and I'll show you a night to remember."

Gibson growls at him. "No. Leave her alone. She's mine."

I am not his but I have to play the part, so I nod in agreement.

Jett's eyes widen. "Does this mean I won?"

My brow furrows. "Won what?"

"Nothing," Gibson insists.

He's cute if he thinks he can distract me. My nickname isn't nosy for no reason. "Tell me more, Jett."

Jett opens his mouth and Gibson releases my hand to jump him. The two fall to the ground as they wrestle each other.

A woman rushes over to me. "What are they arguing about?"

She appears slightly familiar. "Do I know you?"

She holds out her hand. "Indigo. We met outside the bar when you were fighting with your uncle."

"Your explanation doesn't exactly narrow things down much," I mutter as we shake hands.

Two other women join us. "This is Virginia and Leia. Virginia is with Dylan and Leia is with Fender."

Those names I do know since Gibson gave me a rundown on who's who in the band. He couldn't believe I didn't know who *Cash & the Sinners* is. Believe it. I don't listen to rock. Give me country any day of the week.

Leia points to Gibson and Jett wrestling on the ground. "What are they doing now?"

"Fighting over some bet Jett claims he won. Don't ask me what the bet's about." I shrug.

Leia studies me. "Did you come here with Gibson?"

"Yeah. We're dating." I force myself to say the words. This is the agreement I made I remind myself. It's only temporary.

Her jaw drops open. "You're dating Gibson?"

"For more than one night?" Virginia asks.

Indigo smiles. "This is excellent. I knew we were going to become best friends."

"You knew we were going to be best friends?"

"Yep. The first time I saw you. It was best friend at first sight."

It's official. These women are batshit crazy.

I point to Gibson and Jett. "Any idea what they're fighting about?"

Indigo's smile vanishes. "It doesn't matter anymore."

"You just proved it does matter."

"I'm going to tell her," Leia says and Indigo scowls at her. "She needs to know what she's getting herself into with dating Gibson."

Leia grasps my hands. "Don't run away."

"Famous last words," Virginia mutters.

"Gibson and Jett have an ongoing bet on who can sleep with the most women," Leia says. "And by sleep I mean have sex."

"I kind of figured as much," I say while my mind whirls. I knew Gibson was a player when I agreed to this charade.

I didn't know he was a complete and utter asshole. Sure, I suspected. But now it's confirmed.

Strike three. He's out.

Chapter 37

Happily ever after – something Fender never thought he'd have but he's not giving it up

A MONTH LATER

Fender

"This is the last of the boxes," I say as I set the box in the hallway.

Leia glances around her hallway, which is currently filled with boxes. "How do you have this much stuff?"

"Why wouldn't I have stuff?"

"You wear the same jeans and t-shirt ensemble every day. You had no decorations up in your rental house. What could you…. Hold on, is this all musical equipment?"

I grunt.

"I'm assuming your grunt is a yes." She's not wrong. "I know you're a professional musician but where are we going to put all this stuff?"

"We'll leave it in boxes until the extension's finished."

Her head snaps back. "The extension? We're not putting on an extension."

"But you love this house."

She nods. "I do."

"But this house isn't big enough for a family."

Pain flashes in her eyes before she covers it up and wags a finger at me. "I agreed to you moving in. I didn't agree to give you children."

I snatch her hands and draw her near. "I'm sorry."

She blows out a breath. "You don't have to apologize a million times."

"Yes, I do. You're still hurting."

"I need time."

"Okay." I kiss her nose and step back.

She narrows her eyes on me. "Okay? You aren't going to push me?"

I snort. "Pushing you hasn't ever worked before, firecracker."

The fight bleeds out of her eyes to be replaced by warmth. "You're annoying."

I grin. "I do try."

"No using your dimples to get what you want."

She's wrong if she thinks I won't use every weapon in my arsenal to ensure she's happy.

She scans the boxes. "I still don't know where we're going to put all your stuff. My office is basically a closet I converted. There's no other room."

Time to try this again. "Do you like this house?"

She smiles. "I love it."

"Do you want to live here forever?"

"It's a rental."

I tweak her nose. "You didn't answer the question."

"Yeah." Her eyes glaze over as she imagines our future in this house.

"Thus, the extension."

She frowns. "I said it once but I'll say it again. This place is a rental."

I clear my throat. "Actually."

She holds up a hand. "No. Do not tell me you bought this place for us."

I stalk toward her and she retreats until her back hits the wall. "Why not?"

"I'm not with you for your money."

"I know." I tuck a strand of her hair behind her ear. "I was a fool to ever think otherwise."

"At least you admit you're a fool."

"I *was* a fool. I'm not any longer."

"Except you bought this house without consulting me."

"It's my 'we're moving in together'-present."

She rolls her eyes. "That's not a thing."

"Says who?"

"You're annoying."

I grin before I drop my head and brush my lips against hers. "Is this annoying?" I plunge my tongue into her mouth and she grabs hold of my shoulders to hang on tight. I press my body against hers as my cock lengthens and hardens.

This is where I belong. Where I will always belong. Good thing I got my head out of my ass and realized Leia is not Vicki. And she sure in hell isn't anything like my mom.

"Gross!"

At Isla's shout, I release Leia and step back.

"Baby girl," Leia begins. "Kissing isn't gross."

Isla feigns retching. "It is when it's your mom and your dad."

Dad? She considers me her dad? My heart hammers in my chest as I kneel in front of her. "You called me your dad, cutie pie."

"Is that okay?"

"Do you want me to be your dad?" I hold my breath as I wait for her to answer.

Leia moves to stand next to her daughter. Isla glances up at her and she nods. "Go ahead."

"Fender, will you adopt me?"

My chest warms as happiness pierces through me before spreading to the rest of my body. My entire body is alight with euphoria. My hands tremble as I reach for her.

"You want me to be your dad? Forever?"

"Yes. I love you, Fender."

I squeeze her hands. "And I love you." I pause before risking it all. "But I think I should marry your mom before I adopt you."

I hold my breath as I wait for Isla's response. I hope she doesn't think I'm rejecting her.

"Then, ask her already. What are you waiting for?"

I chuckle as I release her hands. I should have known Isla would use the moment to get what she wants. Like mother, like daughter. I dig into my pocket and pull out the ring. When I hold it up, Leia gasps.

"Leia Wilson, will you marry me?"

She raises her eyebrows. Naturally, she's not making this easy for me. Not my firecracker. And I love her all the more for it.

"I wasn't looking for love. I didn't think I deserved it. I never thought I'd find it. But here I am kneeling before my girls asking you to say yes and make us a family."

She drops to her knees and throws her arms around me. "Oh, Fender, we're already a family."

Isla pushes her way in between us. "Does this mean you're going to adopt me?"

"Your mom hasn't said yes yet."

"Mom," she whines. "Say yes already. You love him."

"How do you know I love him?" Leia asks.

"You get googly eyes whenever you talk about him."

Leia giggles. "Googly eyes?"

Isla widens her eyes and bats her eyelashes. "Googly eyes."

Leia tickles her ribs and the two fall to the floor laughing. It's a sight I want to watch for the rest of my life. Preferably with more children. But I can be a patient man. I've waited thirty-two years to find a family. I can wait a little longer to grow it.

There's just one thing missing. I snatch Leia's left hand and slide the ring on her finger.

She stops goofing around with her daughter to smile up at me. "I guess I said yes."

I grunt. "You were always going to say yes."

She shrugs. "Maybe."

"No doubt about it, firecracker."

She rolls her eyes. "Rockstars. Always so full of themselves."

Isla glances back and forth between us. "She said yes. Now will you adopt me?"

"I will." She squeals but I hold up a hand. "On one condition."

Her bottom lip trembles. "W-w-what?"

"You'll call me dad and go to all father-daughter events with me."

"Yes!" she screams and launches herself at me. I wrap her up in my arms and hold on tight. Leia winds her arms around my waist and lays her cheek against my back.

This is it. Everything I've ever wanted but was afraid to go after. Surviving my mother's rants and Vicki's deceitfulness was worth it to end up here. Home. This is home.

Isla pulls away first. "I'm going to call all my friends. Tell them I now have a daddy."

She runs down the hallway and I stand before helping Leia to her feet. She stares after her daughter.

"The whole town is going to know we're engaged within fifteen minutes."

"Do you care?"

"No, but they do have a tendency to invade the house whenever there's news to celebrate." She motions to the boxes. "The house isn't exactly ready for an invasion."

"I'll put these in the bedroom until the extension's finished."

"I agreed to marry you but we're not done discussing the extension."

I bark out a laugh. "Love you, firecracker."

"And I must love you to allow you to bring twenty bass guitars into my house."

"Our house," I correct. "And I don't have twenty bass guitars." With me. "We'll have plenty of space when—"

"If," she corrects.

"The extension is built."

She studies me. "You already hired a contractor, didn't you?"

I shrug and bend down to pick up a box.

"I can't believe you."

"You love me," I sing as I carry the box down the hallway to the bedroom. She follows me with a box of her own.

I scowl. "I told you I'd carry the boxes."

"I'm short, not weak."

We arrange the boxes in the closet before I snatch her wrist and haul her to me.

She shakes her head. "Isla will catch us again."

I drag her into the closet and shut the door behind us. "Not now she won't."

"Fender Hays!" She slaps my chest. "Am I your dirty little secret?"

"Yes, you're a secret. It's why I bought you a diamond to wear in front of the world."

"I do like shiny things."

"And I love you." I brush my lips against hers.

"I love you, too, future husband of mine."

About the author

D.E. Haggerty is an American who has spent the majority of her adult life abroad. She has lived in Istanbul, various places throughout Germany, and currently finds herself in The Hague. She has been a military policewoman, a lawyer, a B&B owner/operator and now a writer.

Printed in Great Britain
by Amazon